BLOOD OF THE PACK

DARK INK TATTOO
BOOK ONE

CASSIE ALEXANDER

WWW.CASSIEALEXANDER.COM

Cover by the Bookbrander.
Interior art by IV Benjamin.
Used with permission.

INTRODUCTION & CHARACTER ART

Angela: I know fear well. It's had me looking over my shoulder since the day I ran from The Pack, Nevada's most dangerous werewolf motorcycle gang. I've had seven years to build a life and my tattoo parlor with the help of my best artist, Jack. But I'm living on borrowed time. My ex-boyfriend may still be in prison, but that won't stop him from getting what he wants — our son.

Jack: I want her, I crave her, but I can never have her. So I wait and watch from the shadows. But when a friend is murdered by the same gang that's threatening Angela, I vow that they will never touch her. Their blood will be mine first.

She's a wolf backed into a corner.
He's a vampire on a tight leash.

Welcome to Dark Ink Tattoo, where needles aren't the only things that bite...

Dark Ink Tattoo is a scorching paranormal in the vein of Sons of Anarchy, with strong sexual situations and bisexual MCs.

Content warnings can be found on cassiealexander.com.

CHAPTER ONE
ANGELA

I heard an engine turn the corner, startled, and the MMA fighter I was touching up a truly regrettable tribal tattoo on yelped.

"Sorry. Spine," I apologized, peeking over his hulking shoulder to see Jack Stone arrive on time for work, possibly for the first time ever while in my employ. His black 1963 Lincoln Continental swooped through Dark Ink's parking lot like a hearse.

Just Jack.

I knew what his car sounded like. Even though our shifts didn't overlap often—I'd heard it often enough to know it wasn't a bike. And still....

I sprayed my client's shoulder with cool water and wiped the blood away, trying to ignore the slight jitter in my hand. This was my job—this was my tattoo-shop—and I'd been doing tats for the past seven years in peace. I breathed deep and willed myself calm. I wasn't scared and I hadn't lost control, and if I kept telling myself that long enough eventually I might believe it.

I put the heel of my hand on the fighter's back to steady it and stepped on the pedal to get the gun roaring again, starting where I'd left off, cleaning up some cheaper artist's shoddy job. In no other profession was the phrase 'you get what you pay for' so true.

This time, the fighter twitched, not me. No way not to hit nerves when you were tattooing someone over bone. Tattoos on top of bone felt like you were getting stabbed.

A lot like getting menacing letters from your ex in prison.

FIVE MINUTES LATER, Jack was leaning over from the wrong side of the counter, purring my name. "Angela."

I didn't turn around. I knew where he was, of course, I'd just made it a habit to ignore him. Mostly.

"Hey, boss-lady, I'm on time, just like you asked," he tried again. I snorted, stopped working, and looked up.

A gaggle of barely-old-enough-to-be-in-the-shop girls flocked behind him, flipping through flash displays, clearly whispering to themselves about him. He was stare-worthy. If you were into tall, lean but muscular men, black hair, brown eyes, and full sleeve tattoos, Jack was your kind of guy. When our shifts overlapped I had to remind myself he was off limits the same way that ex-smokers have to remind themselves to forget about cigarettes. I knew it was for my own good—I'd quit men that were bad for me a long time ago —but that didn't make it any less hard.

It was also why I tried to ignore him. It was good for him sometimes.

"On time for once," I corrected him.

"It's winter," he said, like that was an explanation.

I saw the post office truck pull into the parking lot behind him and my stomach clenched. "Yeah, of course," I said without thinking, standing and pulling my gloves off. "Wrap him up, will you?" I said, sidling towards the hip-high swinging saloon door that divided our half of the shop from the client's.

"My pleasure," Jack said, setting his ass down on the piercing display case and spinning his legs over to switch sides. Normally I'd yell at him about that, but—I reached the door just as the postman did, opening it up to take our letters from him.

Junk mail, tattoo convention flyers, the electricity bill and—something stamped 'Approved by the LVMPD'.

Goddammit.

I bit my lips and ran for the office. I stopped myself from slamming the door, just barely, instead whirling to place my back against it, like that would help keep all the monsters at bay, and slowly sank to the floor.

I threw the rest of the mail to the ground and opened up Gray's letter.

Visit me.

Funny how it only took two words to blow my life apart. I bit the side of my hand to stop from screaming—but somewhere on the inside, a hidden part of me howled.

I tore his letter up—same as I'd torn the other three I'd gotten, starting two weeks ago, and threw the pieces of it into the trash. If only escaping Gray were so easy. I should've left years ago—given myself and Rabbit a head start—but then what? Keep running forever? When I knew Gray and the Pack would always be able to find us? No, instead I'd pretended that I'd had a normal life—that I was normal. I'd rolled the dice, praying that someone meaner and nastier than Gray would take him out in prison.

I should've known that no such person existed.

I'd lived in Vegas my whole life—you'd think by now I'd be a better gambler.

There was a quiet knock on the door behind me. "Boss-lady?" Jack's voice, full of concern.

I stood and straightened myself out, opening the door a crack. "I, uh, didn't know what to charge him—so I asked for two-fifty. That enough?" Jack asked.

It was way more than I'd have asked for. It was only a touch up, hadn't even taken an hour. "He paid that?"

"I can be very convincing," he said, and shrugged, searching what he could see of me with his expressive eyes.

"Stop that. If I wanted to tell you about it, I would."

He leaned forward and pressed the door open. I could've fought back—could've closed the door—but I didn't want to make a scene. But my office was meant for only one person, one desk, one chair, there was no way for us be in here and not be in one another's space. In other circumstances I'd thought about doing things to Jack in here that'd make even the most jaded local blush, but now—I'd much rather he hold me and lie to me that everything was going to be all right.

"What was that?" he said, jerking his chin at the other mail still littering the floor.

"Nothing."

He stared me down. Could he really read me? Or was he just one of those guys who made you think they could? The kind you had relationships with where you filled all the silences with too much hope?

"Seriously, Ang," he said, his voice low.

I gestured to include the entire parlor. "It all says it's for me."

"Even the one from the Las Vegas Metropolitan police department?" he asked. "Don't ask me how I know what stamped mail from prison looks like."

Damn, Jack being Jack. Too smart for his own good. "It's none of your business," I said, as boss-like as I could, shutting down the conversation.

Jack took his cue. "All right, all right,"

"And I need to go."

"Yeah, to your date, I know."

I hadn't told him I was going on a date tonight, that that was why I needed him to really-I-mean-it be on time for once. And he'd said it with almost precisely flat inflection, so I couldn't really tell if he was jealous or whatever—and it didn't matter, because I was with Mark now, anyhow. But some deep and secret part of me bared its teeth and wagged its tail.

He glanced down at the letters. "If anything bad comes of that, you let me know, okay?"

"Sure," I lied, and pushed past him, out the door.

CHAPTER TWO
JACK

I leaned across the counter to watch Angela go. My boss had the kind of ass that made me question my employability on a daily basis. So far I'd been wise enough to refuse to shit where I eat—Dark Ink tattoo was Vegas's only 24 hour tattoo studio, and there weren't too many places where an artistically inclined vampire could work all night for coffin rent. But should the day ever come when I got to quit my current occupation, I was taking that ass with me out the door.

Too bad tonight it'd be wasted on Mark, her boyfriend, who I'd met precisely twice. Judging from his BMW and attitude, he had a casino job, a good one. Which was all the more reason for me to keep my damage to myself. Angela had a good thing going with him—if she was smart, she'd lock him down. People like us knew that second chances didn't knock twice.

One of the girls checking out the flash separated from the herd to come over and give me a megawatt smile. "Hey, you work here, right?"

I turned, focusing my full attention on her. She was maybe

twenty-three, curvy, hair that fell in blonde ringlets down her back. She smiled genuinely at me, in an earnest Midwestern way, and I leaned forward on the counter like a cat spotting a mouse.

Just because I wouldn't be spending the night with Angela didn't mean I'd have to be alone.

"I do indeed. How can I help?" I said, making sure to turn on the southern twang of my childhood as I rose back up.

IN THE END there were just two girls out of five—the blonde, and a brave brunette—who wanted to commemorate their first trip to Vegas on their skin, permanently. The rest of their friends wanted to go back to the strip and hook-up with some guys they'd met last night. The leaving girls whispered lewd suggestions that I had no problem hearing—and kept sending text messages from the parking lot outside until their Uber picked them up, leaving the three of us behind.

"So what do y'all want?" I asked, smiling at both of them, trying my best to seem harmless. I hadn't fed in two days. I could not only smell their blood, but taste the way that sweat pricked their skin in fear—of the needles, not me.

Not yet.

"Just her," the brunette ratted out her friend.

"Yeah?" I focused on the blonde. "Let me see which one you picked."

I walked through the saloon doors over to the panel of flash she'd decided on. A retro-version of the Las Vegas sign. It was Angela's original art, but I'd done it a thousand times, and no one picking flash off the wall thought they were getting a one-of-a-kind.

"I like it," I told her. "If you keep it that size, it'll be a hundred bucks." Neither one of them flinched, good. "Where?" I asked, looking down at the tattoo retracing the lines in my mind.

"Somewhere my parents won't see it."

I glanced up. "I'm gonna need to see some ID."

Blonde was indeed twenty-three, and I had her sign all the normal paperwork, affirming that she wasn't drunk or high, and that she realized letting someone pierce you with needles—with anything, really—always involved some measure of risk.

She signed everything, tentatively at first, then more boldly as she committed to her course of action, and I felt a little like Mephistopheles on a cold German night.

"All right then," I announced the second she was done. "You figure out a place?"

She nodded, sending her curls bouncing. "Here," she said, placing her palm on her hip.

"Excellent location," I said, and held a saloon door open.

BOTH GIRLS WENT to my station without me telling them which one it was. Did it look like me? Perhaps. There were pictures of my art all on the walls. These were my one of a kinds, and once I'd tattooed any of these on someone, I'd destroy the original, or give it to the client to keep. I could do anything anyone wanted me to, being halfway dead had given me the steadiest of hands: American traditional, Japanese, neo-traditional, new school bullshit—but what I loved doing most was photorealism. There was something about photorealistic art that channeled my memories of the sun.

"So—I—" the blonde said, tugging at the waistband of her skirt.

"Yes, please," I said, and handed her some of the paper-clothing that they gave you in doctor's offices, which stayed on exactly no one nowhere.

She pretended to be modest for a moment which I enjoyed, as modesty was a rare thing in Vegas after sundown, then slid her skirt to the floor, kicking out of it, hitching her underwear in and up. I patted the chair and she hopped up onto it. I listened to the leather sigh and sympathized, as I lowered the back of the chair down and the legs up.

I leaned over her. "Okay. First I'm going to shave things, clean things, put the stencil on, and then make art." She'd signed a document saying as much three minutes ago, but people always needed reminding. Something about the adrenaline of knowing what was coming up, and that it would likely hurt, rendered otherwise intelligent minds empty.

The brunette leaned over to whisper a joke about wasn't she glad she shaved elsewhere, earlier, in the blonde's ear, and I hid a wicked smile, before returning with gloved hands and razor.

"Here?" I said, drawing a circle where the sign would be, and blonde nodded. "All right." I drew the razor gently backwards, against the grain of her fine hair. She was holding her breath, and I hadn't even started yet.

"Breathe," I reminded her, and she did, looking flush. Her skin was so pale, the part of her hip she'd chosen nearly translucent, hidden by a bathing suit from her likely numerous summer tans. I could see a trace work of veins in there, more delicate than any art I'd mark her with, and sense her blood pulsing through all of them. Her pulse increased, and the smell of her sweat was sharp and sweet. "All right," I said again, like I was calming a horse, rubbing one gloved hand over the shaved spot to make sure I'd caught everything. Then I set the stencil in place and sprayed water on the back of it.

"A little cold," I warned, too late.

"Feels good," she said with a brave smile. Then I pulled the stencil off and it was needle-time.

I made a show of inspecting my needles with a magnifying lens because I had to, in case any were defective and because if she was going to faint, I wanted her to do it now, before I'd started. She didn't, so I wheeled my work stool closer, looped an elbow in between her legs to brace against the inside of her thigh, pulled up ink onto my needles and pressed the pedal down. I brought my gun hand down and she started whining, "Oh, oh, oh!" at volume. I released the pedal—the needles hadn't even touched her skin.

I looked up at her, "It's not too late. You can still change your mind."

And behind me, the door rang as a new client walked in.

CHAPTER THREE
ANGELA

"Rabbit! Vitamin time!" I shouted. I had gold heels in one hand and an eyedropper in the other. "Rabbit!"

"He's not deaf, you know," my mother said as she rolled in on her scooter—exhibit A in why I couldn't have left town, besides. I couldn't go without my mother—and ever since her hip went bad, there was no where she could go without her scooter. Taking an elderly woman on an interstate trip to avoid your ex-boyfriend's motorcycle gang didn't sound like a recipe for success.

And there was no way I could leave her behind. I knew the Pack. Who knew what they'd do to her to get to me?

"I know he's not deaf, mother, but he still needs his vitamins."

"Those aren't vitamins though. I looked them up online. You keep taking that shit, and you'll turn blue."

"Keep your googling to yourself, all right?" I whispered, then shouted, "Rabbit! Get down here!"

My son tromped down the flight of steps from his bedroom to the landing in our apartment's kitchen. "But Mom," he complained.

"No. No buts. Not tonight. I'm in no mood," I snapped—and regretted it, as I watched him wince and shut down. My Rabbit was a sensitive boy. "I'm sorry. Work was rough—and I've got to go soon. Can you just come here and take these for me?"

He came forward, shy as a kicked puppy. Which was...I didn't want to think about it. He opened his mouth, just out of reach, and I squirted his 'vitamins' in—then got another eyedropper full from the bottle to take myself.

"That stuff—" my mother started.

"When's the last time we ever got sick?—" I said, asking the both of them. "Never. See? They work."

"They make my stomach hurt," Rabbit said.

"Mine too. But it's worth it, okay? C'mere," I said, and ruffled his fine blonde hair with one hand while I pulled a heel on with the other.

"And just what time will you be coming home tonight, Missy?" my mother asked archly. I gave her a glare and caught her grinning. No one could torment you like family.

"Yeah, Missy, what time?" Rabbit caught on.

"That's enough out of both of you," I said, blushing. "The truth is —early, probably."

"What? Why?" my mother cranked. "Rabbit—get," she demanded, and my son thundered off again, back to whatever game I'd called him away from before. "Angela," my mother began anew, in her woman-to-woman tone, "There's no reason to come home early, if you catch my drift."

"I do. It's just that—" I'd thought about it the entire way home from Dark Ink. If Gray knew about Rabbit—then it was only a matter of time till he found out about Mark. And the Pack—the pack was territorial.

So tonight I needed to break up with Mark for his sake. My mother didn't have any idea about Gray or his letters, and I prob-ably should tell her, but I didn't want to lose the last few days of this—us teasing one another, acting like a normal family, warts and all. Mark—he hadn't signed on for this. I needed to cut him loose.

But before I could begin to attempt to explain any of that to my mother, the doorbell rang.

I WALKED OVER, able to beat my mother's scootering handedly, and opened the door. "Hey handsome," I said, unable not to grin.

"Hey yourself," Mark said, giving me an appreciative once-over. I was wearing a cream colored button down cashmere sweater, a gold skirt not much longer than the sweater was, gold heels, and gold everything else—hoop earrings and a series of bangles that began just under the sweater's three-quarter length sleeves.

Whereas Mark? He could give Captain America a run for his money, if Captain America had a little Italian in him. He had a square jaw, piercing eyes that wanted to be amber, and a five-o-clock shadow, no matter the time of day.

"I'll call if I'm late," I called back.

"Don't bother!" my mother shouted back. "Have fun!"

I flushed, grabbed my clutch off the coat rack and closed the door. Before I could take two steps toward him, Mark brought his big hands up. "Let me fix that for you," he said, unbuttoning the top two buttons on my sweater so the dark rose tattoos over each of my breasts could peek out.

"Mark—it's winter," I protested.

"Don't worry, I promise we're going someplace warm."

I slid my arm through his and let him guide us both down the apartment stairs.

I WAS CLINGING to him by the time we reached his BMW. The desert froze at night, and out here in the suburbs you didn't have the build-ings to cut down the breeze. I stared out the window as he drove, catching myself in reflection.

The real reason I wanted those buttons high—and that I was showing enough leg to almost be indecent as a trade-off—was that when I did break up with him—something I would manage any minute now, really—I wanted my tattoos covered. Sometimes when you hurt someone, even for their own safety, they wanted to hurt you back. And I'd been called enough things because of my tattoos, and had had enough assumptions made about the boundaries of my body—I'd learned in tough scrapes it was far better to show blank skin.

"You're awfully quiet," Mark said, reaching over and putting a hand on my knee.

"Sorry. Just feeling sentimental."

He groaned playfully. "Did I miss an anniversary?"

"Not that I recall."

He let go of my knee for precisely long enough to change gears, and then his hand came back. It felt like it belonged there. "What is it?"

One last night. One last time to be normal, with a normal man. Even Cinderella got till midnight, didn't she?

"Nothing," I said, and reached down to pull his hand a little higher up my thigh, giving it a squeeze.

CHAPTER FOUR
JACK

I rocked back on my stool and turned around, fully prepared to tell someone to check out the flash while they waited their turn—but instead I found Bella, wearing one of her off-the-shoulder peasant dresses with sandals that laced up to her knees. Bella the-wanna-be-witch was the only woman I slept with even less committal than I was, and some part of me loved her for that, with abidingly deep irony.

"Hey," I said, standing up and stepping back. "Give me a minute, will you?" I told the girls, snapped my gloves into the trash, and sauntered through the saloon doors.

"Hey yourself," Bella said as I neared, holding her arms out for me. I stepped into them and wrapped my arms around her waist, pulling her near. Her hair somehow always smelled like chocolate, and I remembered the taste of her skin too easily.

"How's my aura?" I asked when we pulled back without parting.

"Black as ever, Jack." Her eyes flashed over my shoulder at the girls behind me. "I see you're keeping busy."

"Gotta pay the rent. And what can I say, you haven't been around lately."

She shrugged one shoulder without apology. "I'm here now. And I need attention."

I pushed one lock of her dark wavy hair back, exposing the glory of her naked neck, and inside my jeans my cock throbbed. Blood was better than sex—unless the sex was really, really, good. With Bella... "Time and place. Name it."

"Two a.m., my house, tonight. And don't you dare be late. My life depends on it."

"Really?" I made sure to hide my smirk. Bella had a shop a few blocks off the strip, a devoted clientele, and she really did believe she was psychic. I made the mistake of letting her read my palm once—saying she was intense was an understatement, which was probably why the sex was so hot.

"Really. That gives you plenty of time to finish up here." Her hand sank between us and rubbed at me through the denim. "Just make sure you save some for me, okay?"

"Always."

She took a step back and whirled, my audience over, and walked straight back out Dark Ink's doors.

I watched her go, because how could I not, hoping my hard-on would subside. When it didn't, I gave up and walked back to the girls I'd abandoned and sat down. Work would straighten me out, like always.

"Sorry about that," I said while pulling on fresh gloves.

"Girlfriend?" the brunette asked.

"It's complicated."

"Oh," said the blonde, daring a glance below my belt.

Precisely. "You ready?" I asked both of them, since the blonde's tattoo seemed like a team sport.

"Yeah," Brunette answered, and took the Blonde's hand. "Come on, Karm—you can do this."

Bolstered by the brunette's encouragement, the blonde chimed back, "Yeah—I can." Except for when I set my gun hand on her she let out a high pitched shriek—and once I pressed the pedal and the gun started roaring, so did she. Consent paperwork be damned, anyone that walked into the shop right now would think I was killing someone.

I knew first-hand what that sounded like.

I rocked off the pedal, staring at the blonde over the plane of her pale stomach, meeting eyes briefly with her best friend, before looking at her again.

"Look, can you take this? I don't want half-finished flash out there with my name on it."

Blonde Karm—short for the Karma I'd seen on her license, which I'd copied to prove her age—nodded vigorously.

She wanted it too. And I wanted money. But unless she'd let me actually tattoo her, we were at an impasse. I could use my whammy —it was the Jedi mind-trick vampires had that got people to do things for them, like open doors and invite them in—but it wasn't very strong or useful yet—not like my Mistress's. It'd gotten Angela an extra hundred bucks for her touch-up, earlier, but I'd seen the way that MMA fighter was also looking at her ass—I'd just charged him an ass-tax was all. But using it to get someone to sit still for a tattoo that I wasn't sure they were really into wasn't worthwhile.

"Why do you want it? What are you commemorating anyhow?"

Karma pushed herself up on her elbows. "I just—wanted to prove that I was here, you know? It's my first time out of 'Bama."

I knew I knew that accent. And I knew all about how easy it was to get stuck in the south—and how hard it was to leave behind, no matter how hard you tried.

"I might not get to make this trip again," she went on, looking up at me with wide and innocent eyes. "I want to make it special."

And there it was. Everyone who came to Vegas was looking for the same thing—to go home with a good story.

I sat there quietly for a moment, lips smugly curved, looking from one to the other of them. I could feel the tension building between us, almost thick enough to feed off of. "If you don't want to get a tattoo, I can think of several other things to do that you'll remember forever instead," I said, offering everything they thought I was.

Karma's lips parted as she inhaled a gasp, then her eyes darted to the brunette, as if asking permission. The brunette's eyes flickered over me and she subtly nodded, and then Karma nodded too, more strongly.

"All right then," I purred, and made it my mission to get Karma to scream again. I raised the chair she was in to be head height to my stool, and wheeled myself up between her legs. I pushed the paper away, and pulled the cotton line of her panties to one side. I could feel her eyes on me, both of them scared but entranced.

"You're—you're going straight down there?" Karma whispered. Her hair was trimmed in a neat landing strip—what a shame that someone who groomed themselves so neatly couldn't call it pussy.

"I am," I said. "And she's going to start kissing you."

Karma looked to her friend, whose name I didn't know. The brunette blinked once, twice, and laughed a little nervously, but then leaned in and tried. Their lips mismatched, they both laughed, and then tried again, this time with better outcome, as I watched Karma's breasts heave.

I didn't need to whammy them, they just needed a little orchestration—it was likely the first time they'd done this sort of thing, much less together. Wanting to do my part for the tourism industry, I put a warning hand on the inside of both of Karma's soft-skinned thighs and then lowered my mouth down.

Karma was wet, she was warm, and I slid my tongue between her folds just tasting her as she moaned into the brunette's mouth. The brunette slid a hand under Karm's shirt and underneath her bra, and I could see her kneading Karm's breasts while I licked up toward her mound. I was warming her up, kissing everything, rubbing in with my lips and chin, I wanted her to know that I was here, and I was into her, and then I opened my mouth wide to suck on her clit, that way that women liked, that most men never learned.

She started to make high pitched sounds between kisses, and I saw the brunette's hand find her nipple and pinch, and then Karm's hand was reaching out between them until it found a home between the brunette's thighs—she rose up from kissing, panting, pulling her own skirt up and her underwear down so that she could stand with her legs wide enough to give Karma's hand room.

I sucked on Karma's clit, rolling it under my tongue, rocking my head forward to give my gloved hand space to rise. I put two fingers into the warmth of her vagina, but didn't press them in—instead I pulled down, so she would feel stretched and empty and yearning. Karma rolled between our attentions, her free hand clenching onto my tattoo chair's side, her hips rocking beneath my ministrations, the brunette pushing Karma's shirt and bra up at last to kiss Karma's perfect breasts.

"Oh my God, y'all—oh my God!" Karma shouted, and I felt her tense, her thighs trapping my head, as I kept sucking, and then I slid my fingers in and—"Oh my God! Oh my God! Oh my God!" she kept shouting as her orgasm shuddered though her, up and down, her hips spasming, her stomach pumping, her breasts bouncing with the force of it, until she finally sagged back with a final whispered, "Oh my God."

Her thighs relented and I pushed back, my face covered in her juices, eyes blurred with a contact high. I fed better when I did more fucking, but life was life, and she had come hard, giving everything to me.

The brunette stood, panting, her legs still tight around Karma's hand, and cast darkly inviting eyes my way.

I slowly stood. There was no way she couldn't see my hard-on straining against the denim of my jeans. "Do you want a story too?" I asked, my voice like gravel and full of promise. She reached for my belt buckle without answering.

She—she knew what was going on. She'd done this before—I could tell—from the way she rubbed at my cock with her hand through the fabric of my jeans, then after she'd unzipped the fly, the way she reached in to feel it again, as though weighing it, comparing it to some unmatched part of herself. I groaned until she undid the top button and let my cock fall out, aching.

If I'd known her better—or at all—I would have run my hands into her hair and brought her head lower—I wanted to feel her soft red lips wrap around my shaft as I slid into her mouth and down her throat—but as it was I had to wait till she got there herself. She knelt slowly, stroking me, until her lips were at height and—she looked up, and licked them, then parted for me, taking the head of my cock into her perfect little mouth, and beginning to work her way higher.

As she started riding my cock with her mouth I shuddered. Sex— made me hungry—and here I was so close to blood—but—no— hands were in my hair—Karma, back from the dead and standing, pulling my mouth to hers, kissing me. I ran my hands over her soft skin, clawing fingers up her back, pulling her against me as my hips fucked her friend's mouth, until I found her nipples, pinched, and pulled—then the brunette rocked back.

I looked down at her, my cock still ramrod straight—and she whispered up. "Do you have a condom?"

I moved Karma aside and pulled one out of a station drawer, opened it and set it over my cock with practiced hands. Then the brunette stood. Her hair was in disarray, which gave her a chance to hide behind it as she asked. "I want you to fuck me—but I have to stay a virgin."

It was all I could do not to laugh. "Southern girls," I said aloud. I kicked off the rest of my clothing and grabbed the Vaseline from my drawer and brought it near. We used it on fresh tattoos, but it'd do for lube—and the condom was for them, not me, besides. The upshots of being a vampire included no babies, and no STDs.

I lowered the tattoo chair and then settled myself on it, my back against it, as its back was tilted down. I was face up, hips up, and my aching cock was still at attention. The brunette gave me a quizzical look, which was a shame—after the virgin quip, I wouldn't have thought she suffered from a lack of imagination. "Come here," I said, grabbing her bodily and pulling her up to lie on top of me, her back against my chest, her legs splayed wide, dangling on either side of my hips.

I pushed her hair away to nuzzle her neck and brought my hands around, one to cup a breast, the other pushing down through her dark fur to stroke right above her pussy.

She was helpless on me. I was bigger than she was and totally in control, and I could feel her torn between fighting that and giving in. I used the wetness Karma had already inspired to rub her labia gently, feeling them part, then pulled up to find the space where they connected at her hood. And I started slowly arching my hips, sending my trapped cock rubbing against the cleft of her ass.

"Just don't—go in there—okay?" she whispered, setting one hand on top of mine on her pussy to guard it, and bringing her free hand up to play with her other breast.

"Understood," I whispered into her ear before licking the shell of it, making her shiver. "Karma, can you do me a favor?"

"Uh huh," Karma said, watching everything with rapt attention.

"Take some of that," I said, jerking my chin at the Vaseline, "and get it all over my cock."

She breathed a yes, and went to do as she was told—then paused in front of us, looking down at where we almost met, at both of us, and I wondered how much, if anything, she'd learned in sex ed—or if she'd ever gone to the dark side of the internet.

Then she reached in and pulled out my still condomed cock and slicked it up and down with Vaseline thoroughly, giving it a solid stroke that made me growl.

"Okay," I told the two of them, pulling the brunette higher up my chest. "You ready?"

She nodded and I started my slide, pushing her slowly down as my hips arched my cock up. Her hips bobbed in time with my other hand, but when she realized what I was doing, where I was going, she started to move to find me. I was pressed against her in a moment, the head of my fat cock rubbing against her tight asshole, and then I whispered, "Breathe for me."

She did, I thrust, and I pushed my tip inside her. She moaned and I went still. She was throbbing around me and I could feel all the blood racing inside of her as she processed the moment. "You good?" I asked, the fingertips of one hand playing gently with her clit.

She gave a small nod, and answered, "Yeah," right before trying to squirm down.

"Good girl," I purred, and arched up to make things easier for her.

I listened to her moan with pleasure as her ass took more of me inside. She was tight, God *she was tight*, and it was hard to just wait for her to find her own rhythm—but before I could break she did, and started riding on me, back and forth, sliding me in and out each time she squeezed her ass and arched her hips, slowly taking more and more of me in each time.

I pinched her nipple and then my hands sank to her waist without thinking, dying to help her, wanting to land myself inside her to the hilt, even as she worked her own way there.

"Christ," I growled. She may not have done this much before—but she was good—so good—I opened my eyes and saw disheveled Karma, watching us intently.

"How can I help?" she whispered.

I reached both hands over the brunette's body, spreading her legs even wider, showing Karma her full sex. "Sit down on the stool—and suck her right here," I said, showing her where with a finger.

The brunette paused in anticipation of Karma's mouth and then afterwards let out a low moan. She lay between us, pinned and twitching, scared of moving too much and knocking anyone off.

"I can't—decide—it all feels—so good—" she panted out against me.

"What feels good? This?" I said and finally pushed up, making her take all of me at last, feeling her stretch around the thickest part of my shaft.

She grunted and then moaned, wrapping an arm up to run her fingers through my hair.

"Or this?" Karma asked, getting into the spirit of things, licking harder, taking more of the brunette's pussy inside her mouth.

I decided to take control of the ride then—just because I was technically immortal didn't mean I wanted to play all night long—and I had other dates besides. I curled up, taking the brunette with me, pushing her down, feeling her welcoming ass handle my girth.

I twitched inside her, arching my ass up, rocking myself just barely in and out of her as her whole ass clenched me tight, making each small thrust feel like the first time.

"Oh God," she moaned, as her body betrayed her. She reached out for support and found Karma's head and brought her in, so that we were both bucking into the other girl's mouth.

"Yes, yes—don't stop, oh God—please!" she begged the two of us, as I felt the beginnings of her orgasm wrap around me, like the calm before a storm. She was going to give it to me, give it good, and I was going to fucking take it from her. She moaned, thrashed, and then began to scream, as her ass spasmed around my cock and pulled.

"Fuck, yes." My fingers grabbed her thighs and held her down as I pumped up, bucking my hips against hers as she writhed, pounding her with my release as her life pulsed out of her—I held her close and took it into me, feeling it warm me deep inside, just like my cum was now heating her. I rode her until we were both finished, and growled again with one last thrust.

I held her close as she panted, worried she'd fall off the chair if she tried to move—until Karma's head dropped, as she started to lick at my balls.

"Goddamn," I said, releasing the brunette slowly. "You're going to make someone very happy someday. You both are."

The brunette dizzily dismounted, turning to lean against the chair as Karma stood. "That was wild."

"Yeah, it was." I sat up, twisting towards them, watching them find and straighten their clothes as I sat naked as a jay-bird, with the exception of my tattoos, a huge skull on my chest, and a dragon trailing over a shoulder, with both arms sleeved. Now and again, one of them would look shyly at me, as if to convince themselves that that had happened, that I did exist. All I could do was smile back.

When they were almost pulled together, I stood and made a show of stretching before expertly tossing my condom in the trash. Two semi-innocent southern girls and add in a little Vegas, and look what I had done.

"Was that a good enough story for you?" I asked.

Karma looked dismayed, and for a half-a-hot second I doubted my skills. "But we won't be able to tell anyone."

I laughed. "Those stories are the best stories." I swooped down to grab my jeans as the brunette leaned over to whisper something in her ear.

"Jennifer!" Karma said, scandalized, then grinned, and took her hand. So the brunette's name was Jennifer. I slid my jeans on as they gossiped. Who knew what the rest of the night would hold for them, if they played their cards right. And hey, now they could always play with each other.

"We've, uh, gotta go—" Jennifer said, tugging Karma towards the door.

"Yeah, I figured," I said, buttoning my jeans.

They turned and dashed out with victorious laughter, already telling each other the story of the story in their minds—how brave they'd been to go get tattoos—and everything that'd happened after. What I'd done to them, what they'd done to each other, and the sanitized version of events that they'd tell their friends while secretly giggling.

The door rang again as I was putting my shirt on. Jennifer stood outside, hailing a ride with her phone, but Karma'd bounced back on through. She raced up to the counter and slammed a wad of cash down.

"Since you didn't get to tattoo me," she said with a grin—and then disappeared back outside.

I could've chased after her—there was time before their ride got here—but with the people I owed money to, I couldn't afford too much pride.

Besides, no one could say I hadn't done my part for Las Vegas tourism for the evening. It was every local's duty—even the undead ones. I fastened my belt buckle with a smirk, and pocketed the cash.

CHAPTER FIVE
ANGELA

"We're going to the Fleur de Lis?" I whispered as Mark drove us up to valet. It was Vegas's newest hotel, the swankiest one yet, built just a year ago. He'd told me to dress up tonight, but what I had on wasn't going to cut it –

"The one and only." Mark hopped out of the car and tossed the valet his keys, then held my door open.

"What about—" I said looking back, expecting him to do the usual and tell the valet his name and phone number—to at least get the chance to ignore the 'we are not responsible for your belongings!' on the back of the card.

"No time, come on," Mark said, tucking his arm under mine, propelling me forward.

When you live in Vegas your whole life, you get jaded, quickly—you get the kind of eyes that see the dust in corners and cobwebs too high to reach. You knew there was a man behind the curtain—hell if you worked for the casino, you were the man behind the curtain—and it helped you blink the diamond dust right out of your eyes.

But all that said—the Fleur de Lis was legit. Seemed legit. I was... going to have to do some rigorous exploration, once I figured out where the hell Mark was taking me. Please let it be a bar, please let it be a bar—I didn't think I could break up with him if there was a whole restaurant with fancy waiters watching.

"Have you been here before?" Mark asked, after watching my neck turn again. Who knew there could be so many chandeliers and that they could all sparkle so brilliantly?

"No. It's beautiful." Everything was rococo—or St. Petersberg, circa Catherine. It would feel overwhelming if the space wasn't so huge—instead all the ornamentation invited you to look up. It was the kind of art that would make a small person feel smaller—but a grand person, moreso. And sure enough, I felt tiny under the weight of so many frescos and angels and sculptures gazing out, whereas it finally seemed like Mark was at home, the lion in his ornate den.

He caught my chin and brought it back toward him. "Not as beautiful as you," he said, kissed me gently, then pulled me gently toward the casino floor.

I trotted alongside him, two of my steps for each of his normal ones, catching gambler's glances as we passed by. Some stared at Mark, some stared at me, and others were too entranced by the dealers, women wearing low cleavaged Marie Antoinette-style ball gowns, situated behind each table—or looking for the cocktail waitresses, who were also wearing ball-gowns, but much narrower, with ruffled cut outs in the front, all the better to show off shapely legs, ending in appropriately ornate heels.

Mark chuckled as I slowed him down again. "I'll give you the grand tour later—it's just that I'm late—"

"For what?"

"There you are! Marky!" Another huge man loomed out as we went up three stairs to a cordoned off zone.

I could not imagine my Mark as a Marky. Not now, not ever. But the newcomer clapped his arm across Mark's back with a solid thud and then looked at me. "And who is she?"

"Dante, this is Angela. Angela, Dante."

Dante was every bit as big as Mark I realized, as he stepped back to give me a once over—not even trying to hide that he was, as he spun around me.

"It's the eyes or the hands," he explained. "I figured I'd use the eyes, since Mark was here and all." Then he looked to Mark. "Nicely done, brother. Not that you ever pull badly."

Mark cleared his throat loudly and Dante made a somewhat apologetic face, then caught my arm. "I'm afraid we're running behind—so if it's OK with you, Angela, I'd like him to seat you back with all the other good luck charms tonight."

I looked to Mark and he nodded. "Sure," I answered, completely unsure what the hell was happening, but letting Dante take me away.

We went down what I was fairly sure was a service corridor, although the paint and brocade didn't end—perhaps all the better to remind employees just who they were dealing with and how they ought to act at all times—until we reached a quiet room with about fifty seats in the form of assorted velvet lounging couches and a large viewing screen. Dante let my arm go with a flourish and then left, abandoning me with fifteen strangers.

Looking around—I felt like I'd walked into the pages of a fashion magazine. There were women here wearing shoes that cost more than my rent. If I started to calculate how much their jewelry was worth—I stopped, because it'd explode my mind.

I tottered over to the nearest empty couch, feeling awkward like a newborn foal, and sat down. A woman came up to me. "Cocktail?"

"Yes please. Vodka tonic."

She circulated quickly and returned. I took the drink and fumbled in my clutch to pay her, but she shook her head. "Oh no," she said, with a French accent. "Your money's no good here."

Just as I was about to ask why that was, the screen turned on. The Fleur de Lis's logo appeared—a camera shot focusing in on one diamond until it exploded under the pressure into the tri-fold name-sake of the hotel—and then it cut to a room with seven men and three women, all holding cards. Mark was among their number, sitting behind a high stack of chips.

"What the...."

A beautiful woman sat down beside me. She had light brown skin and her dress was a shimmering gold with cap-sleeves. It sank between her breasts almost as high as it cut up her thigh, and her hair was a forest of ebony pincurls. She was outrageously beautiful and secret parts of me wanted to purr. "First time here?" She spoke with a real French accent—which made it all the easier now to identify how fake the cocktail waitress's was.

"Yeah," I said, timidly.

"Ahh." Her lips pulled back in an expansive smile. "Welcome to being a bird in a cage then."

"I'm sorry?"

"This room is soundproof, and what do you call it—" she waved a bored hand. "Electricity proof? The cage—invented by Faraday."

I blinked. "Why?"

"When the stakes are this high, there can be no cheating. We're allowed to see, but not communicate with our loved ones outside." On the screen, the dealer started dealing, and the woman leaned closer to me, clinking my glass to hers. "Drink up."

The other 'good luck charms' and I watched the first hand. I knew they were playing poker—once upon a time I'd dealt it—but what I didn't know was how much each of the chips they were throwing around were.

I had a feeling I didn't want to know, as I watched the first round and saw Mark turn five of them in, as a dapperly dressed gentleman closer to the screen clapped.

"Which one is yours?" the woman beside me asked.

As if to help me, the camera suddenly panned in, showing off the way Mark's brow crinkled in thought at seeing his new cards. So many tells, I could see them from here—didn't he know better?

What did it matter though—it was his money. *And I was breaking up with him besides.*

"Him."

"Ooooh, he's a pretty one. What a jaw," the woman beside me said.

I twisted to scan the room with all of its delicate decorations on the walls, the marble slab table which held caviar and seventy-year old Glenlivet, the pretty people bending and whispering to one another, with sudden bursts of applause as each round ended. This was the kind of place that Gray wanted to burn to the ground. It didn't matter how big Mark was—he couldn't save me.

And when I finished turning in my seat I saw her there, still staring at me. "And—and you?" I said, and took a sip of my drink, hoping vodka would help everything.

"That man in the corner," she said, pointing with an outstretched hand. He had to be over three times her age, maybe four, and I couldn't have pointed to the bottom of his chin or the beginning of his neck. "The one who looks a little bit like a wrinkled sock."

I inhaled enough vodka to burn as I sputtered, "Excuse me?"

The woman laughed. "I'm allowed to say it. Tonight's a night for honesty."

"Yeah. It is," I agreed, and took a much larger sip of my drink, this time making sure not to laugh.

She smiled again. "So how much have you bet on your man? I know it's gauche to talk about, but I'm bored." I gave her a blank look as she went on. "Unless you bet on another one of them?"

My jaw dropped a little. Had the doors of this hotel taken me to an alternate reality? I hadn't had that much to drink—unless someone had spiked me.

"Don't be shy," she encouraged, "I bet against my man all the time."

"I—I have no idea what you're talking about."

"Oh, you are *so* new," she said, and I got that distinct feeling like I was in high school all over again. "They bet on the game and we bet on them, so on and so forth. This is being televised all over, for those who follow such things. Keeps life random. Makes things fun." She rocked back into the couch. "There's no point in living without gambling."

The crowd applauded another round, and the camera scanned past Mark. His stacks of chips were greatly decreased, and if I understood her properly.... "That is some Hunger Games level bullshit, right there."

She tilted her head sharply. "Hunger...Games? But no one here is hungry."

She was definitely having fun at my expense. Had to be. "I'm sorry, I—" I said, and began to stand.

"Don't go," she pleaded, her expression was genuine.

Since this was likely the last time I'd ever be in this room, I asked: "Nothing personal, but why the hell are you hanging out with me?"

She snorted, then lifted one of the sleeves on her shoulder. Underneath was a faded tattoo, murky with time, but definitely of a fleur de lis. She tapped it with one finger, and then looked knowingly at my cleavage, where the roses I'd wanted to hide peeked out, thanks to Mark. "I'm sorry if I upset you. I was hoping to find some companionship. These people," she said, swirling her glass to include the rest of the room, "They buy art. We are art. It's a subtle difference."

It must be so hard to be incredibly rich, sexy, and lonely. I stopped myself before my eyes rolled, sitting primly on the edge of the couch, and trying to be clinical. "I take it you had that before the hotel?"

"Far before. It's an original, you could say."

Her dress did hide it—I wondered if she had to hide it with all her fancy clothes. "You know—tattoo removal's come a long way."

"Oh, I could never get it removed. I need something here to remind me of home."

"Not to judge but—you could cover it up. Or get it touched up, make the lines crisp and firm." I reached out for her shoulder. "May I?"

"Certainly," she said, turning slightly. As I traced the outline on her skin she shivered, and arced her neck to look at me alluringly. "You—your touch is electric. Has anyone ever told you that before?"

"No," I said in a stern tone. But it wasn't the first time I'd had clients try to come onto me. "I could clean it up, nice and easy."

She took my hand with her hand, smiled, and her eyes widened like pools for the unwary. There'd been a point in Rabbit's life when he'd watched The Jungle Book incessantly, and I realized hanging out with her this closely was like staring into the eyes of Kaa. I heard a distant smattering of applause, as if others in the room were cheering, her leaning forward and –

"Angela!" Mark said, appearing in a door. I startled as he walked over, and the woman I was with acted like nothing untoward had happened.

"Mark," I said, stumbling up in relief. "I'm so happy to see you."

"Rosalie," the woman beside me finally announced, standing to introduce herself to the both of us. "Your woman is irresistible."

"Practically magnetic," Mark said, clapping my ass and then pinching it, where she couldn't see. I swatted his hand away—I just wanted to escape.

"Are you done?"

"I am. And so our date begins, at last," he said to me, and to her, "I hope you have a lovely stay."

"Oh no, darling, I'm a local," she said, and blew me a kiss as Mark pulled me out.

I MANAGED NOT to yell at him until we'd gotten in the car. "What the hell was all that?"

"A favor for a friend. They had a late cancellation and needed someone to fill the seat. I finished as quickly as I could. We have reservations at Celestial tonight—we can still make them if we hurry."

It took me a moment to parse everything. "Wait—you lost—on purpose?"

"Did you think I played poker that badly?" he looked over at me with a wild grin and pulled onto the interstate.

"I don't know what to think." The acceleration of the car pushed me back. "How much money was that?"

"Just fifty grand."

I gasped in horror. He was a man that fifty grand was nothing to? I put fingers to my forehead, trying to stop an oncoming migraine.

"You okay?" he asked.

"Please take me home."

He took the next exit and started driving much more slowly. "Why? What'd I do?"

I twisted in the seat to look at him. "It's nothing you did—it's who you are."

"Oh, no—Angela, I know tonight was ostentatious, but—"

"And who I am," I said, talking over him. "We're two very different people, Mark. This has been fun, and I really like you but—"

He pulled over. We were on a backroad, one of the ones that led to a subdivision that'd never been built. "I know what you're trying to do, Angela. Don't. Don't you dare decide things for me."

"We're different, Mark." Now that we were off the strip I could see the moon in the sky—enough of a sliver to feel its pull. "You don't know what you're getting into with me. You think you can handle everything because you have money, but I have problems that money can't solve."

He didn't say anything—he just got out of the car and walked around to open my door for me. I got out and grabbed my clutch as an after-thought, I'd be calling a car if I had to, no way I was walking home in these heels.

The night wind was strong but he shielded me, standing right in front of me to stare into my eyes. "Do you, or do you not want to be with me?"

The moonlight made his features cast strong shadows, and I remembered the way his stubble felt against my thighs. He wasn't going to give me up easily, and inside me a tail thumped with misplaced pride. My wolf had gone and found another alpha. *Goddammit.*

"I do, but I can't."

"Then—just give me twenty-four hours."

"A day isn't going to change anything."

He came in closer. "This day will."

And then he was so near and he smelled so good and this might be the last chance I had to get properly fucked, under the moon no less—I leaned up and kissed him, hard. He tensed in surprise, but then kissed me back just as fiercely and instantly closed the space between us, pressing me against the hood of his car.

His hands were all over me, up my sweater, beneath my bra, and mine were just as eager on him, pushing inside his suit jacket to slide between buttons. I needed skin, skin to skin to skin.

His mouth moved to my neck as I gasped for air, bending backwards under his attention. The wind swept past him and I shivered. "Here," he said, pulling his jacket off quickly, setting it around my shoulders. "And now," he demanded, spinning me around to face the beemer. With one broad hand he pushed me down, bending me over the warm hood of his car. I felt my skirt crawl up my hips and was not even the least bit ashamed.

I heard a zipper, and felt him hitch my skirt even higher, exposing me to the entire world. Then his hand reached down and pulled the thin cotton line of my panties over, running his fingertips against my seam to find the beginnings of my wetness, and in a second his thighs were matched to mine and he was shoving his way inside.

I groaned low. He wasn't afraid to be rough, which was just how my wolf and I liked it, and he knew it. He pushed once, twice, and then it was all over as a flood of my juices soaked him, allowing his cock to ram its way inside. I grunted as he thrust deep and moaned. I loved knowing he needed to be inside me, and I loved being full, and no one else had ever filled me up like him before.

"Oh, fuck me," I whispered, as he grabbed both my arms and hauled me back onto his cock. He thrust hard and fast and then stopped, leaving me aching for more.

"Do you feel that, Angela? How hard I am for you?" He punctuated each of his questions with a thrust.

"Uh huh," I panted, nodding helplessly against his car.

"Whatever it is you're scared of," he said, taking slow, deep, strokes. "I'm not. I feel this, and I know we're supposed to be." He pulled his cock almost all the way out, and teased me with the head of it. "And I know that you need me," he said, pushing all the way back in fast, and I moaned. "I belong inside you. And you belong wrapped around me," he said, and after that started fucking me properly, long and slow.

My heels already had me teetering forward, ass high for him. He slipped his coat up, and smacked it, then dropped the coat back in place so I wouldn't get cold. Then he did it again, on the other side, and I knew I'd have red handprints on my ass till dawn. I couldn't move against the car hood, but I—twisted and got my panties just right, so that each time he thrust they tugged against my clit and— "Mark," I whispered, clenching my hands.

"That's right," he said, arcing himself deeper inside me at feeling me build. "You feel so good, Angela. And I know exactly what you want." He reached forward and grabbed my hair, yanking my head back, so I would feel ridden. I pawed out on the hood, bracing myself for his cock, trying to take all he had to give as he began speeding up, each of his thrusts filling me, winding me. Heat built inside my hips like it was desert sun on a summer day. He reached down and smacked my ass again, harder, as I started shamelessly moaning in time with his strokes.

"Oh God, Mark," I hissed, my breasts rubbing against the hood, my hands clenched into impotent fists. The smacking sound of him taking me rose up into the night, followed by his pleased grunts each time he fucked me good, his thick, hard cock stretching my swollen pussy tight—followed by more spankings—as my panties ground against my clit—I didn't know which was going to make me come, only that I *had* to. "Fuck, yes, fuck!" I shouted as his cock shoved in and pushed me over. I curled helplessly forward, shuddering against the hood of his car, as my orgasm wracked through me.

"God, yes," Mark grunted, riding himself into me, his cock plugging me tight.

I shuddered repeatedly, speared by his cock, feeling it pulse deep inside me as he filled me with cum, but before he was finished, he swept forward and grabbed me, sending his coat fluttering to the ground. He hauled me up as he pushed his hands up my sweater, showing my breasts to the moon, and I howled.

CHAPTER SIX

JACK

Dark Ink was supposed to be open 24/7.

That was part of its 'mystique', and the introduction to many of its favorable online reviews—"Just when I thought I wouldn't be able to get a tattoo!"—but what was understood by me and the other artists who took nightshifts waiting for not-entirely drunk walk-ins, was that you could close up for a few hours here or there. Some of them slept in the back—one of the reasons the bell over the door was so loud—others took naps in their cars during breaks.

As Vegas was between major conventions, it was a weeknight, and colder than balls on a brass monkey outside, I felt pretty safe taking off for a few hours as long as I was back to high-five someone on the early crew pre-dawn. So I drew to entertain myself until one AM, but after that I set the 'be back soon!' sign to a generous five AM and locked the shop behind me.

I walked out to my car feeling loose and tingly. Tonight I was playing close to the edge. Not with my employment—Angela would never fire me, I was the best artist she had—but with my need to feed. I was down two nights, and the co-eds had helped, but I was too hungry for them to top-off alone.

You see, sex took the edge off and amazing sex could just about replace it—and sex with Bella was almost guaranteed to be amazing. But if she wanted to do other things for some reason, like just read tea leaves, my hunger and I were going to have a bad time of it. I didn't turn into a slavering monster after one night, or even two or three, but after four or five I had a lot of sympathy for junkies.

MY FIRST STOP was my apartment. It was a basement unit, next to no windows, perfect for me, antithetical for the majority of Vegas. I slid out of my clothing and into the shower, washing the scent of tonight's Penthouse letter away, and when I got out of the shower, dried off.

I didn't look at myself in mirrors much. Not because I couldn't see myself in them—I could, movies were stupid—but because there wasn't much point. For the past four years I hadn't changed. But now something compelled me to lean over my sink and look. I had one Japanese sleeve, with a dragon swirling up it from my old mentor, the other was covered in thick-lined American traditional tattoos. The knuckles of one hand had the letters JACK tattooed across them, the other had ROCK, since my last name was Stone, from when I was punk and seventeen.

I wasn't stupid, I knew I was good looking, but there had to be something else. Karma, Jennifer, Bella, Rose, Cymberly, JJ, Kate, Ruby —all the girls that'd come before, and all ones I knew would come after—what was it they saw in me? How come with them it was so easy?

Why couldn't Angela see whatever it was?

I pushed back. That was a stupid question to ask and it didn't deserve an answer. Didn't need one. All those other women, they

knew trouble, were trouble, or were just passing through. Angela...
was real to me.

Which was why I wanted her—and precisely why I could never
let that show. I locked down that train of thought and threw away
the key, just as my phone buzzed on the counter.

Bella: Don't be late.

Never, I texted her back, and went for the bathroom door.

BELLA LIVED OUT IN SUMMERLIN, in a suburb that'd sprung up and
managed to thrive. I drove the way to her place by memory and
when I got there coasted in, parking beside her Kia in the driveway.
That someone who considered themselves so mystical lived here and
drove that? I shook my head as I walked up.

Five minutes early, I decided not to ring the doorbell, and instead
just tried the door. It opened—and as she'd already invited me in
once before, and I stepped through.

"Open sesame," I announced, in her entryway/den. Her couches
were black velvet, her lamp had a maroon sheet over it to tint the
light, and everything else was painted black, the walls, her shelves,
her fireplace. Everything but the carpeting was gothic—it was still
its original suburban tan.

"Jack!" She walked in from her kitchen. She was wearing an
apron and not much else, if I could believe my eyes. "You changed,"
she said.

"Not really," I said, giving her a feral grin.

She chuckled and walked around behind me to lock the door.
Definitely just an apron. I started to feel a lot better about getting fed
tonight.

"So what's going on?" I asked, following her back to her kitchen. "It's been months."

"Miss me?" she said, looking over her shoulder, as she returned to stirring a small bowl.

"Always," I said, but she made a demurring sound.

"You know better than to say things you don't mean."

From behind her, the apron covered nothing, which meant that I could see it all: her perfectly heart-shaped ass, and half of her numerous tattoos. She had a tramp stamp from before their coolness came and faded, only hers were photorealistic antlers, coming out of a mystical grail. We'd met when she'd walked into the shop and needed a mandala tattooed on her inner thigh, which led to the first of many times we'd fucked. I could see a hint of it right now, my art, on her.

"Sometimes," I said, more truthfully, walking up to stand behind her. Whatever she was stirring looked like dirt mixed with different dirt. "I'd just assumed you'd moved on." And I wasn't the calling type. Why should I be? I had nothing to offer a normal human being.

Her stirring slowed. "Well, I did. But—it didn't work out. So—now I'm back. But I need your help." She set the bowl down and twisted around to face me. "I'm in trouble."

I set my hands on her hips. "What kind?"

"I—fell in with these guys and—" she started, then looked up at me and gave up. "Your aura's the only thing that's worse than theirs are."

One of my eyebrows rose. "Is that supposed to be a compliment?"

She looked innocently at me—as innocent as she could. "It means I think you're the only person that can save me."

Instead of asking 'Really?' I had the wisdom to growl, "How?"

"Like this," she said, drawing near and leaning up to kiss me.

Bella and I—we weren't kissers. I was generally worried about inopportune teeth and she usually wanted me to fuck her fast and animalistic. So I stiffened as her mouth met mine and her lips parted.

"Bella," I murmured, trying to pull up, but her hands caught my head and brought my mouth back to hers. "What's going on?" I asked, as she set my forehead against her own, giving me a glorious view down the front of her apron at her heaving chest.

"I am," she whispered, and grabbed my belt.

In a moment my belt was unbuckled and my button-fly undone. One of her hands pushed down as the other one went up my stomach. I pulled my shirt off quickly, giving her more access to skin, as her hand inside my jeans found my hard cock and wrapped around.

"You have missed me, haven't you?" she said.

I ran a hand into her thick hair and pulled her head back so she had to look at me. "I'm gonna show you just how much."

She shuddered, at my tone, at my raw need—I saw her do it, and I felt her hand tremble, holding me.

"That's what you want, isn't it?" I said, taking a step forward, still holding her by her hair, pressing her back against her countertop. "You thought you were going to be in control tonight, didn't you?"

She nodded a little, her head unable to pull much against her trapped hair.

I lowered my head to breathe in her neck, to smell her, to almost be able to taste her blood—to definitely be able to taste her sex, in the wetness that I knew now freely flowed between her thighs.

"I don't know who you've been fucking, Bella, but they sure as hell weren't me." I stepped back, letting go of her hair and pulling myself away from her in a rush. "Take that apron off, now," I commanded, and her shaking hands went for the knots. "Then get back to your bedroom and lay down, ass up."

Her eyes widened and the apron fell to the ground as she raced down the hall.

I TOOK my time in her kitchen, kicking off my boots and my jeans. I knew she could hear me, just as I knew she'd obeyed. She wanted something from me—and I needed something from her. Waiting made it sharper for us both. And before I walked after her, I went to the den and grabbed the scarf from her lamp.

Her room was even darker than the den was, but vampires have excellent night vision. Although if I hadn't been able to see her, I'd still have heard her, breathing unsteadily as she waited and hoped, and I'd definitely have been able to smell her, anywhere. I walked up behind her bed, which she was on, ass up, like I'd commanded. I put my knees against the mattress, moved it, and heard her gasp.

"Jack?"

I held the scarf up between my hands. I hadn't decided what I'd do with it yet. Maybe I ought to gag her. "Yeah?"

"I'm scared."

"Whoa." I stepped away from her bed, letting the scarf go. "Why? It's just me." We'd played rougher games than this before.

She turned on the bed, laying naked in tousled sheets. "It's just—I was supposed to—the past few months—they've been really bad for me." She got the words out in gasps, and I realized she was crying.

"Oh—Bella." My hard-on sank, and my hunger lunged out, like a dog on a leash. She crawled across her bed to me and pulled me down to hold her. "I'm sorry," I apologized, for who or whatever had hurt her. "I am sorry," I said, brushing her hair from her face.

She clung to me, sobbing, and all I could do was hold her back. "My poor baby," I whispered to her, like someone long ago had once whispered it for me, and rocked her, skin to skin.

"No, I'm sorry," she said, wiping a hand across her face. "I didn't mean to do this with you."

I could feel her heart beating against the wall of my chest, and felt small fangs budding out. "You can't be strong all the time. It's okay."

She looked up at me and put a hand to my chin. "How can you be so evil and still be so safe?"

I was taken aback by the question. Did she know what I was? How could she? "I don't know," I said, and tried to blow it away.

She ran fingers through my hair, scratching my scalp, sending tingles down my spine. "Maybe you're not evil yet is the thing. Maybe all of your evil is still to come."

"Maybe," I said flatly, hoping to discourage further conversation.

She inhaled deeply and pulled back, looking straight into my eyes. I didn't know what she was trying to find there—or if the man in the mirror that answered so many women's unspoken desires was looking back. Then she moved in—I thought to nestle herself against me again, and I started bargaining with my hunger, swearing to give it fresh blood tomorrow night—when I felt her lips kiss at the hollow of my throat.

I sat still, not wanting to scare her, not wanting to assume. Her lips trailed down a half-inch to my sternum, and kissed me there again.

By the time she reached my navel I was panting. I didn't want to —I wanted to be in control—but the hunger—knowing where her lips were going and why—there was no way not to be hard. But as her lips met the light hair trailing down to the base of my cock I found some inner reserve I didn't know I had, and stopped her. "You don't have to, Bella. I'm here for you. Without that. Really."

"I know. That's why I'm doing it," she whispered, and her mouth sank onto my cock.

I groaned and slowly fell back on her bed, as her mouth overcame me. There was enough light for me to see her but I still closed my eyes, giving into the sensation of her tongue against my head. She stroked the tip of me with it and sucked just the head gently, cupping her lips all around. I wanted to buck up and make her take more of me, but I could already tell—if we fucked this time—the way we were going to fuck—it'd shut my hunger right the hell up. All I had to do was hang on.

She worked her mouth down my shaft and started stroking my balls and I risked thrusting, feeling my cock bend down the back of her throat, held in tight. Her dark eyes looked up at me, waiting, and for the second time that night I reached for her hair—to push it out of my way so I could see her. She purred at being watched and went faster—and my body and my hunger fell out of sync. My body wanted her to taste me, now, to hold her head and thrust until every-thing was spilled inside her mouth. But my hunger required much, much more to be sated.

I pushed myself up on my elbows. "I need to fuck you," I growled.

She pulled herself slowly off my cock, letting me feel each inch revealed, and then looked at me, breathless herself. "So do it," she said, her voice just as low, and I took it as a challenge.

I folded over myself and grabbed her, pulling her over me, shoving her up, until her thighs framed my face. I knew she was wet, but I had to be sure—I grabbed her ass and pulled her onto me, burying my face in the sweetness of her pussy. I licked her open and pushed in and felt more than heard her moan, her whole body shud-dering over me. I worked my tongue up until it was under her hood and sucked at her there, while pushing my chin up to grind. I felt her ass tense under my hands and she rocked against me, begging me to suck harder, push deeper. More wetness flowed, so much, and I knew —I pushed her to the side, so that I could get out from underneath her. I had to get my cock inside her—now. I rose up behind her, her on her knees in front of me. I grabbed her hips and pulled.

"Jack," she hissed, as my cock landed. We both waited there for a moment, feeling this new space, occupied. Her breath hitched and then she rocked against me, and I thrust into her, and we were off again. I saw her dart a hand down between her legs as I hunched over her, thrusting deep and I braced with one hand and wrapped the other around her, holding onto her breast, rolling a nipple. Each time I thrust she grunted and soon both her hands were on her head board, so she could press back into me. I felt my cock glide in and out of her on a river of juices and spit and thought maybe I'd never been so deep in a woman before—maybe I'd finally met someone able to take me—the hunger roiled through my body, fusing with it, becoming one with all my motions, so that all of me was ready to devour her the second she–*let–go*–her pussy swelled and grabbed my cock and I knew—I grabbed her hips and thrust wildly, shoving my cock in and out, feeling her thick walls close in as my hard cock arched up and—Bella screamed as the first wave clenched tight.

Luckily, I knew her—I knew so much better than to slow down.

I fucked her right through that orgasm, and the next, and the one after that—it was like she had a switch inside herself that, once flicked, wanted to stay on—her pussy like an incandescent light. By the fourth one though—my hunger couldn't stand it any longer. I'd absorbed so much life from her, but none of it would count if I couldn't give her some back.

"Bella, baby," I warned her, and somehow through her orgasmic haze she managed to brace herself again.

"Give it to me, Jack," she begged, her voice rising, as she started to clench again.

I—if I hadn't made sure she was wet—if I hadn't felt her clutch my cock before—I might have worried about the ferocity with which I fucked her now. But no matter what I did she took it and then I felt her pussy grab greedily on, like she was trying to suck me dry—

"Goddamn," I moaned, and thrust deep one last time. My cock rammed inside her, and then and only then, did everything spill out. My body shuddered as I moaned but I kept her on me as I spasmed, pushing my cum as deep as it would go, claiming her for me as her pussy milked me tight.

She fell forward, and I fell on top of her, still inside her, both of us throbbing. The hunger was gone—would be gone—for the rest of the night. If I could only fuck her every night—I pulled her to me— but she struggled free.

"Don't go," I complained.

"I'm not. I promise. I'll be right back."

She pulled away from me and off my cock as I sighed. Reality came rushing back, brushing away foolish dreams. What time was it? My phone was in my jeans back in the kitchen.

"Don't go anywhere!" she shouted.

"Where would I go, woman? You've fucked my dick off," I shouted back, and heard her laugh. I looked down at myself, at my fat cock slung to one side. It's a good thing I was immortal, or that might've been the truth.

She returned, naked and gorgeous, holding the bowl she'd been stirring when I'd first walked in. She put her finger to her lips for my sake, and then began casting a spell—something Latin-y about binding and safety and protection. I tried not to look bemused.

"There," she said, when she was done, and had painted a half-circle of the bowl's contents on the floor around the bed. "Now you're mine."

"Hmm?"

"I used some of our juices to bind you to me. Now you're not allowed to leave my side." She set the bowl down and fell back into bed beside me.

I tilted my head. I didn't feel any different. But I was also still on the inside of the circle. "Don't good witches usually ask permission first?"

"They do, but desperate times and all that."

I traced a hand down the side of her body. "You know you could've just asked?"

"It's not like you exactly come when called, Jack." True. "And anyhow, it's temporary," she went on. "I only need protection for a few days. After that I'll be fine. I've seen it in the cards."

I opened my mouth to tell her all the reasons I was unreliable, namely that I died with the rising sun. But I knew that'd sound stupid and she wouldn't believe me, or worse she'd ask to see, and I couldn't just show that to her. There was no other vulnerability quite like dying by someone.

So what I said next was, "Okay," even though I knew it was wrong, and pulled her to me. The sooner she thought I was trapped the sooner she'd sleep and I could leave. I brushed her hair away from her face gently. Maybe she could come to the shop tomorrow night, if she was still speaking to me then, or I could get the night off —but there was nothing I could do for her during the day—she'd have to go with non-magical 911. And I couldn't tell her a thing.

"Bella," I began, trying to come up with a good—*any!* —explanation.

She reached up and bopped me on the nose with a fingertip. It smelled like wet dirt and sex. "Shush. It's done. Just go with it. Your boss is too into you to fire you if you take off a few nights. I've seen that too—so don't worry."

Not for the first time, I wondered what went on inside her head.

"And tomorrow we can go by the shop and get your gun—I want these gone." She pulled back from me and lifted a breast, showing me a new tattoo I didn't know she had—six paw prints, wolf tracks, running underneath.

"A cover-up?" I made a show of pursing my lips thoughtfully. "I'll see what I can do," I said, and pulled her even closer. "Go to sleep, silly girl."

"Did I wear you out?" she asked disingenuously, snuggling up, tossing a leg over my thighs.

"Always," I said. I kissed her forehead, and then stared at the ceiling until I heard her snore.

CHAPTER SEVEN
JACK

Bella's room had black-out curtains in true Vegas style. I had an amazing sense of time—and I could feel mine slipping away. It had to be almost pushing up on five. I'd spooned Bella until she'd overheated and rolled away from me, and I hadn't chased her across the bed.

What was I going to do with her? I guess it depended on how much she hated me. I'd find out tonight.

I crept out of her bed and walked up to the line she'd drawn. I didn't feel anything. I waved a hand over it, and then I hopped over it entirely. Whatever magic—if any—she'd mustered, didn't work on me. I wondered if any of her 'magic' worked at all. I knew there were powers at large that most humans didn't dream of—and I also knew if I ever told her I was a vampire, she'd go from the wild thing she was to some kind of groupie.

I backed away from the bed, waiting for her to wake up, and when she didn't, I headed into the kitchen.

I GOT DRESSED in the entryway, popped the bottom lock on her door so it'd latch behind me, and then made sure it was after I closed the door, quietly testing the lock. It was solid—and when I looked at my phone I realized I was late.

I drove faster than I should have to get back to Dark Ink, guilt over leaving her chasing me—and the knowledge that every minute longer I was gone was one I might get caught. As I pulled into Dark Ink's parking lot I was almost as surprised to see Mark's BMW there as I was to see Dark Ink's ornately painted front windows, shattered.

Mark and Angela were standing in front of the damage. I leapt out of my car and slammed the door, running up, as Angela whirled.

"Jack!" Angela shouted, and stormed over to me. She was beautiful, she was always beautiful, but this time—her skirt wasn't more than an inch down her hips and her sweater-top was unbuttoned almost down to her navel—she was sex on wheels.

"You!" she started, looking from me to the building. There were tears welling in her eyes and she raised her hand up to hit me.

I caught her wrist before she could—and a shock permeated through me, a whole-body lightning, like the bangles she wore had turned her arm into a battery. I stiffened, transfixed, then let go.

"Sorry—" I apologized, as Mark loomed.

"No," she said, taking her arm back and touching it where I'd touched her. That shock—had she felt it too? Then she ran a hand through her tousled hair. "I don't normally hit my employees—I just —I thought you were dead!"

I looked back at the front of the shop. "It'd take more than a little broken glass to kill me."

"The alarm company called—you were supposed to be there!"

"We get lunch breaks. Look at the sign—" I pointed, and prayed she couldn't smell the sex on me, like I could so clearly smell on her.

Mark cleared his throat. "All right—about this," he began and went for his phone.

"What're you doing?" Angela said.

"I'm calling the cops. And a repair shop."

"Don't do that."

Both Mark and I looked at her. I was glad, I didn't want to get tied up here too much longer, dawn was on the way—but this was clearly the act of vandals.

"Just—let me clean it up," she said, and started over into the glass, teetering on her heels. Mark gave me a man-to-man look then.

"Angela," I started, walking after her, "It's my shift. I've got this." I could call in some favors. I had an hour. And the dawn crew would be in shortly. "Go home."

I reached her side and saw her crying, tears flowing down her face—but the entire rest of her body, the way her jaw was clenched, the set of her shoulders, her hands in fists by her side, said she was ready to attack. Crying—but angry.

"Angela, come on," Mark said, rounding her up. He weighed twice what she did, he could pick her up and carry her out of here if he had to.

"I've got this," I promised again, and she flashed me a look, nodding once, then followed Mark back to his car. I waited until they drove off, then I pulled out my phone.

DAWN CREW WAS new artists who had to take what shifts they could get, and Mattie, who in another life had clearly been a farmer. I called all of them first, rousting most of them from bed, and Mattie arrived earliest like he always did.

"Hey!" he shouted from outside. "What the hell?"

"I know." I'd collected the biggest shards into the trash, and had been working with a broom and dust-pan for half-an-hour. The glass had gotten into all the couch cushions—we'd have to go after them with a vacuum.

"Anything get stolen?"

"Not that I could tell." They hadn't taken the iPad we used to charge our clients, or broken into the office for the cash drawer. Everyone's kits looked secure.

"Weird," he said, stepping through the window to join me.

Mattie started his morning routine, making himself coffee with the hot water spigot and his French press, and turned on the radio, as I stood looking out the broken window. The neighborhood we were in wasn't great, but it wasn't bad either—and on a chilly night like last night, most people would have had better things to do.

So was this personal? One of the newer artists? People generally didn't become tattoo artists because they played well with others. I couldn't help but think of Angela, barely clad and standing there pissed. Mad because it was her business that'd been attacked? Or mad—because it was a message meant for her?

Just like the one I'd seen her get from the LVMPD?

The jangly rock song on Mattie's station ended, and the morning DJs took over.

News fresh from Summerlin—a violent murder on the corner of Verdant and Ambrosia. The victim was Bella Wintermichael –

The broom I'd been holding clattered as they went on, and Mattie emerged from the back. "Jack? You okay?"

I didn't answer him as the DJs went on describing the scene. It must've just happened, mere minutes after I'd left her.

"You've had a long night," Mattie said, coming up.

"You don't know the half of it," I said, remembering Bella's worried eyes.

He clapped me on the back. "Go home. Get some rest. We'll get this cleaned up, me and the boys."

I nodded, and walked out to my car in a fog. *Oh Bella, what did I let happen to you?*

Bella had chosen me to protect her, I'd ignored her, and—what if she'd been right, and I was the most evil thing in her life?

I'd figure out who she'd been scared of—and I'd make them pay in ways they never dreamed. My hunger pulsed inside me like a super nova. It'd been so long since I'd let it go—but at the thought of the carnage I'd wreak on Bella's behalf, my fangs began to bud.

A piece of glass outside spun away from my boot, distracting me from my bloody daydreams. I watched it twirl, then knelt down to pick it up—it had a flourish from Dark Ink's blue and gold letter D. I'd never forgive myself for what'd happened with Bella—but if anything happened to Angela—my hand tensed and the glass nicked me. I watched it bleed for a moment, then threw the glass far away before bringing my hand to my mouth. I never wasted blood—not even my own.

And tomorrow night I'd be drinking someone else's.

CHAPTER EIGHT
ANGELA

I sat down in a plastic chair on the other side of a bulletproof window and held a phone to my ear. "You wanted my attention. Well now you have it."

Gray, my ex-boyfriend and my son Rabbit's father, sat on the other side, holding his own phone to talk to me. "Hey, baby," he said, grinning broadly.

I waited there to see what he'd say next. I didn't want to give him anything. They'd taken my coat, but I made sure what I was wearing showed neither curves nor skin. And my expression was flat. He was nothing to me. And there was nothing he could do to me, behind bars—which was where he was going to rot. Forever.

Except a month ago he'd started sending letters—and last night, he'd sent someone to bust the windows of the tattoo studio I owned, I was sure.

"You look tired," he said. "Long night?"

There was a point in time when I would've thrilled at his concern. When I'd been eighteen, when I'd started running with the Pack, when I'd seen him—I knew I'd had to have him in that obsessed-teenager way. That my life wouldn't be complete without him. He was six-four, broad-shoulders, Viking-arms, and—yeah, given my now-boyfriend Mark I clearly had a type.

But Mark was a lawyer, not a drug-dealing-murdering-son-of-a-bitch-behind-bars who I hated every day.

I crossed my legs and stared off into middle distance, ignoring him. I knew he hated that. As leader of the Pack, he expected utter loyalty—and with the exception of me, he'd mostly gotten it. Werewolves and bikers had an inherent sense of hierarchy.

"Angie," he said, his voice just a croon, the husk of his wolf coming through. He knew what I had inside me, how much the wolf-part of me still wanted to please him.

"Don't try," I told him. "It won't work."

My wolf was a fickle bitch. Luckily, I took silver every day, so that I was always the one in control. I'd learned it from the Pack—smuggled colloidal silver into prison was the only way Gray could stop from wolfing-out on moon-nights too.

He leaned back, surveying me. "I just wanted to see you again, Angie. That's not a crime."

"Breaking Dark Ink's window is."

"If I did that, it's just petty vandalism. Plus I'd have had my guys make sure no one was inside. All completely theoretically, of course."

I gestured to myself. "Well, you've seen me now. I'm going to go," I hung up the receiver and brought my eyes up to stare at him blankly like he didn't count.

He waited until I'd almost stood to ask, "How's my son?" I didn't hear it, so much as I read his lips through the glass.

Blood rushed in my ears. If I could keep going, walk on out like I hadn't heard him—but I'd waited half a second too long, and we both knew the truth. I sank back into the chair, trying to appear indifferent, and when I picked the phone back up I made sure to say, "What?" in an incredulous tone.

Rabbit was the only good thing to come out of my time with the Pack. And when I'd gotten out, I wasn't even late yet—and then he'd been born late, besides. There was no way they could know anything for sure, unless—

"I'm not stupid, Angie. He looks just like me. I have photos."

Bile rose at the thought of some drug-running biker following my son around with a camera. "Rabbit isn't yours. He's mine and some other guy I fucked. I fucked a lot of guys after you. Still do."

"Looking for a cock big enough to replace mine?"

"Hardly," I laughed sharply. "Let's just say that when you're not a virgin, you have a lot of catching up to do—and that those experiences put earlier ones in... perspective."

He was still looking at me with that trademark killer-grin. "I'd forgotten how feisty you were."

"Did your masturbatory fantasies leave that out?"

Gray leaned forward. "I know you're afraid of me, Angie. I can see it in your eyes. You don't have to be."

He'd left me alone for seven long years, until last month. Maybe he'd changed behind bars. Found Jesus, or Buddha, or whatever.

He put his hand up to the glass and tilted his head. "I just want to be a family again."

And at that, I laughed loud and true. "Are you fucking kidding me?" His eyes went cold, like a predator's, and I remembered just how hard he could hit. "He's not yours," I repeated.

"Cut the crap, Angie—unless you want someone to help me get a DNA sample."

I froze. I wasn't sure what I was more scared of for Rabbit's sake —him finding out that he was a werewolf—or that he was related to Gray.

"Being in here," he said, knocking on the glass between us, "has given me some perspective. I know now I never should've let you go."

At that—all the anger and all the memories came rushing back. "Like you let Willa go? And all the girls before her? Fuck you, Gray," I said low, this time with my own wolf's voice, and watched him startle. "Fuck you. You knew she might die—that I might die—and you never said a word."

He leaned forward on his side of the glass. "I didn't need to say it. I wanted you to be my mate for life. I wouldn't have knotted you otherwise."

"That was supposed to make me feel special?" I forced myself to laugh hollowly, to hurt him, even though there was no way I could ever hurt him the way he'd hurt me. "After you left—do you know what Wade did?" I swallowed down the stomach acid that rose as I remembered the night. I'd only come back to the bar for my tattoo guns—they were Dringenbergs, practically irreplaceable, as I didn't have a penny to my name, and doing tats was the only way I could make any. And that was when Wade had stopped me. He just picked me up and carried me off to the back room, me screaming the whole time. "He took me. Carried me off to your room—our room—and threw me on the bed. Said he'd waited long enough, and it was finally his turn."

Gray's jaw tensed and his eyes narrowed, and I knew no matter how in control he was of the Pack that no one outside had ever had the balls to tell him this story. Or, none of them had ever thought he would care—one of those two. I leaned in.

"I could hear the rest of them through the walls—so I knew they could hear me screaming. Trying to fight him off, kick him away. And when at the end—when I was covered in claw marks and bitten— when his knot finally flared and trapped me there, on him, him touching me, holding me for half-an-hour while he whispered apologies to me for what he claimed his wolf made him do, begging me to stay? I will die before that ever happens again." I stood. "Maybe Rabbit is his—but I know he's not yours, and I'm definitely not your mate. Don't ever contact me again."

I dropped the phone and walked away.

"What're you going to do when the moon calls him?" Gray shouted after me. I ignored him and kept walking.

CHAPTER NINE
JACK

I woke like I always did—to the sound of scratching against my coffin.

I wasn't in a coffin because I was a vampire—although I was—I was in a coffin because I'd acquired a cat, and an EMT client of mine had once told me a horrible story. I kept Sugar well-fed, but when you died each day and shared the house with a carnivore, it paid to play it safe. I heard an inquisitive meow, and another scratch right by my head. Somehow, Sugar always knew when I was up.

"Shush," I said, pushing back the lid of the plywood box I'd built for myself. Sugar jumped inside and rubbed her head on my hand, as I knuckled between her ears.

The only upshot of being a vampire was that I didn't dream—I could never toss or turn while I slept, when I fell dead I stayed dead, until sunset. I could count the number of people that'd seen me dead on one hand, including Sugar, and I wanted to keep it that way.

But if I'd still been human I knew what I would've dreamed of— blood. Both to drink—and to see spilled. Whoever had killed Bella had to pay.

I reached for my phone with my free hand.

My first text was from Mattie, telling me a new window'd been successfully installed at Dark Ink—but that Angela had cancelled nightshifts until further notice. That was worrisome, as I still needed the income—but it proved that she was scared. I'd have to ask her why, but tonight off might be fortuitous, because my next text was a half hour old, from Paco.

Free?

Yeah, I texted him back. Hopefully he hadn't made other plans—but he knew the rules I played by. *Can I bring OJ?* Our code words for if I could bleed him. If I couldn't I might have to make other plans—the kind of things I wanted to do tonight required blood.

Only if you bring Oreos, he texted back. I smiled darkly at my phone. Oreos were everyone's favorite post-bleeding snack.

Done, I sent back and sat up inside my coffin, already beginning to feel more alive.

I SHOWERED and drove out to Paco's. He lived in a fancy mansion at the edge of town, one with an infinity pool and a view of the mountains. It wasn't his, it was the magician he was monogamish with, but the magician left town pretty often—and the last time he'd done a tour on a cruise I'd pretty much moved in, Sugar and all.

I parked in the driveway and grabbed the Oreo's I'd promised, walking up just as Paco opened the door.

"Jack," he said, smiling at me. He was as tall as I was, wearing loose shorts and a tight white tee that showed off all his muscles. Every time I saw him I remembered the first time we'd met, when I'd lured him into a club's bathroom to bleed, and wound up fucking him instead, both of us twined inside a tight stall, me pounding him as the dance music pounded the wall opposite. "How is it that we both have the same night off?"

"Don't know, don't care," I said, dropping the cookies to the ground before reaching for him.

Our mouths met as I pressed him up against the wall of his entry way. My needs tonight were savage, stabbing me from the inside out. I leaned my whole body against his, running one hand up his shirt, using the other to twist the waistband of his shorts and pull him toward me, as my tongue pushed deeply into his mouth.

He shivered, a full body thing, not just due to the night air I'd brought inside with me. I knew he cared for me, and I for him, and yet every time we met I knew he couldn't help but remember what I was—even if I'd promised I'd never bleed him without warning. I pulled back, biting on his lower lip, rocking my hips against him. "Sorry," I apologized.

The corners of his lips quirked up into a warm smile. "Don't be," he said, and his hands reached for my waist.

Our hands were all over each other's bodies—there was no place that Paco wasn't perfect, I knew because I'd kissed them all before. In moments our clothes were tugged at, then off, and kicked aside, and we were stumbling naked, mauling one another. He pushed me towards the hallway to the bedroom, but that was too far—I shoved him towards the living room.

I kissed him hard, then pulled back again, both our cocks were hard between us, and seeing his—I reached down and glided my hand over his cock's silky surface, watched him shudder and heard him purr.

"I love your cock," I whispered, as I pressed him against the high back of his boyfriend's designer sofa.

"Jack," he whispered back, his breath warm against my ear, my name an invitation.

I let go and spun him, then pulled him back against me, so he was trapped, both of us staring through immense windows at the moonlit desert night.

"Nothing out there is as beautiful as you." I licked up from his shoulder to his ear, and he reached up to claw his hand through my hair. I waited for a moment, relaxing into the feel of his back against my chest, the way our bodies were perfectly aligned, the scent of his sweat mixed with mine. I kissed his neck again, then his shoulders, slowly kneading his broad back down to his ass until I pressed my thumb against his tight asshole and rubbed it there, making him moan.

"You want me in you?" I said, running my other hand up his muscled back. I replaced my thumb with the head of my hard cock, using my hand to rock it over him.

In short answer, he spread his legs and pressed his hips back. I spit into my hand and slicked it over my head and shaft—and in long answer, as I put the head of my cock against him again, he hissed, "Yesssssssss."

Despite the urgency of earlier, I went slow now. I leaned back and watched myself enter him, bit by bit, feeling his ass envelope me one millimeter at a time. He tried to push back harder, but I stopped him with my hands. "Patience," I warned, as he moaned in disappointment.

It felt like I was diving into a pool of velvet, cock-first. As badly as I wanted to fuck him—and I did—I wanted this slow sensation more, of pushing myself into him, feeling him slowly take me, stretching to let me enter. I knew the rewards I would reap if I took my time, and him too, no one I had ever bled kindly had gone unsatisfied. I brought my hands up, around his neck for a moment, then down his shoulders and back, to his waist, and then up again, as my cock pushed further into his ass, until we were hip to hip and close enough to dance. His hips rocked against mine, unable to wait, and one of my hands found his waist, the other, one of his shoulders, and pulled him back into me.

"Goddamn, Jack," Paco groaned, feeling me swell inside him, his ass stretched at my cock's widest point. I pulled out fractionally, then pushed back in, the motion I'd made taking him in reverse. "Jack," he gasped after a few short strokes, "I need more."

"Good," I growled, and gave it to him.

I pushed him down and over the sofa's far side, clawing my nails down his back, and started fucking him in earnest, pulling my thick cock out of his ass and then pushing it in again, each of my strokes answered with moans. He pressed himself up and straddled his legs wider, trying to take more of me, while my cock pulsed in him, hard and straight. I'd needed this again—almost as much as I needed blood—this was the only time I felt alive—I pulled myself all the way out of him, as he groaned, and slapped his ass hard once, before picking him up and tossing him over the back of the couch to bounce back-down on the other side.

"Jack!" he protested.

"What?" I said, coming around from the left. I clambered over the arm rest and shoved foolish cushions out of my path, crawling towards him with my cock slung low. I grabbed his knees, pushed them out and open, and pushed myself back in his ass. He growled and I moaned and then we moved as one.

We'd been together too often not to have a rhythm, and now we found it, all over again, my cock deep in him and my balls slapping against his ass with each stroke, him raising his hips high each time to let me in. His hands reached in to pull at his own hard cock but I pushed them away and spit into mine again to lubricate it—I wanted to feel him fully, inside and out, and started to slow my thrusts to give him time to catch up. Between the head of my cock pumping against his prostate and me jerking him off, he had no choice.

I heard his breath hitch and felt him tense, starting to writhe— his thrusts were shorter now, more desperate, and I knew he was gritting his teeth to stop from begging me for release.

"Just say it, Paco."

He looked up at me, a lock of sweaty hair over one eye. "Never."

"Fine then, I'll just fuck it out of you." I started moving all of my body in concert, bracing myself over him with one hand, my own sweat dripping onto him, his legs on my shoulders, him curled beneath me as I thrust harder, me stroking his cock with an expert hand. I'd stopped searching for my own release and segued into wanting to play him to find his—he was so close to breaking, and he was so beautiful when he did –

His whole body tightened, stiff as a board, his ass clenching my cock hot and hard as his own cock ramrodded through my hand, and then he shouted, almost a scream, as I felt his ass pulse around me and my hand fill with his warm seed.

I kept fucking him then, through the best of it, and then more gently, to land him safely on the other side, both of us collapsed on his couch.

"You didn't come," he complained, as my cock slid out of him, still hard.

"I will," I said, pushing his damp hair back, laying down on the wide couch beside him. I brought up my free hand and licked his cum off it.

After all, life was life.

When he'd caught his breath again he rose up on one elbow, facing me, stroking a line up and down my chest to my stomach. My erection sank and subsided, leaving me with a panging ache. "So what's going on?" he asked.

"Can't a guy just need some blood some times?"

He smiled down at me, then leaned in for a fast kiss. "Not when that guy's you."

I stared up at the tastefully vaulted ceiling overhead. "A friend of mine got into some trouble. And died. Because of me." I told him all about Bella, how we'd fucked and then she'd wanted me to spend the night to protect her. He groaned at that, knowing who I was— and groaned even more once I told him she'd been murdered after I'd gone.

He stopped petting me. "You know that's not your fault, Jack, right?"

"It sure as hell feels like it."

"You couldn't have stayed."

"I know. But—I still feel responsible." I twisted my head to face his. "And I'm still going to punish whoever did it. As soon as I find out who they are."

Paco's dark eyes searched mine, and his hand on me started up again, stroking lower and lower. "And here I was, hoping you'd spend the night."

"Sorry to disappoint you. Again."

"Jack, you're a hell of a lot of things. But you've never been a disappointment." And his hand reached down to ring my soft cock and I gasped gently. Then he leaned over and kissed me, first my eyes, then my nearest cheekbone, and licked my lips to let his tongue inside. My lips parted just as my cock stirred—his fingertips were stroking the edge around my head, feeling me, exploring me, just as he stopped kissing my mouth and started working his way down my neck.

It was my turn to whisper his name. "Paco." Why hadn't I come inside him? He'd wanted me to—I'd wanted me to. I hadn't even bitten him yet and—his hips rocked against mine as his hand around my cock pulled it firmly—possessively—and that was it. I'd already lost one person close to me—in the cat-like way of closeness I allowed myself, now that I was this. If I was, as Bella had so often claimed, bad luck, I couldn't stand it if anything of me harmed Paco.

His mouth was at my collarbone, kissing me where I wanted to bite him. "Paco," I warned again.

"Shut up, Jack," he murmured from against me. "I know you." His moving hand sank to stroke my balls and rub the soft spot between my ballsack and my asshole—and the hunger rose in me and—I twisted toward him, bringing his face up to mine with both hands to kiss hard. He purred as my body pressed against him, my cock rising up between us like a cobra. I pushed it down as I lowered myself, my skin sliding on his still slick with sweat, needing to angle myself into him again. I grabbed his top leg and pulled it high over my hips, then cupped his ass as he thrust toward me and my cock sank into velvet again.

He moaned as I pushed in, and my cock felt like it was home. "God, Paco."

"I know," he said, rocking off and on.

It was impossible not to look at him this way, to see the earnest intensity of his eyes, how much he trusted me, how much he knew I'd always make him feel good—even if it hurt a little along the way. I kissed him then, under his jaw, against his chest, anywhere I could taste him, I craved it almost as much as I craved blood—

But not quite.

The hunger—I could feel my own blood rushing inside my veins, as much as I could feel his, it was like our hearts were timed, counting the same beats as my cock fucked his ass—my fangs descended and I panted, "I'm gonna," I warned.

"Do it," he said—and I did.

On an upward thrust, as I was claiming his ass again, I bit down. There was an art to it, I didn't want to damage him, I only wanted him open—as open to my mouth as his ass was to my cock. I bit down, then latched on, clutching him bodily, feeling him spasm with the pain even as he knew it was coming, then the taste of his hot, hot blood spilling into my mouth, so indescribably intense—my cock got so hard in him it felt like it might burst if I didn't come right then and—

For a perfect moment we were like some holy circuit, me drinking life out of him while I pounded more life in, my cum shooting deep with each thrust and spasm—and I went somewhere else. That place you only reach at the peak of certain highs, when you feel invulnerable, when talking to God and flying seem possibly real, a sharp clarity on everything in life—and then I sank back to Paco's couch again, where his hands were clenched tight, one in my hair, the other on my ass, him grinding himself against me, until he moaned and spasmed around my softening cock. "Good," I whispered, knowing he'd cum again—I could smell its earthy scent and felt the heat of it between us as it tried to stick us together though our breaths fell out of sync.

I lifted my head up from his neck, my lips rimed with his blood. "Thanks."

He looked down at me, his own eyes glazed. "You're welcome," he said, and I sank my head back down.

CHAPTER TEN
ANGELA

I stalked back to my car in the parking lot. Something about being near Gray had pulled my wolf to the surface, and she was as pissed as I was—with me, for Rabbit's sake? Or against me, for leaving Gray? She was such a separate thing from me, I never felt like I could control her, and I had no idea.

I sank into my beat up Honda four door and tried to push her down inside. Her being so close frightened me, which was why I kept a small bottle of colloidal silver and an eyedropper inside my glove box. I opened it up, stirred around inside for it, didn't find it, tossed everything out, becoming frantic—it had to be here somewhere—I started looking underneath the passenger side seat, and then my own, and missed an officer walking up to me till he tapped on the driver side window.

"Ma'am, is everything okay?"

I startled, guilty only of looking guilty, like I was searching for drugs or a gun, and rolled down my old-fashioned window with the crank.

"What do you want?" my wolf growled at the man. And then, as if startled at the sound of her own voice, she left me. His eyes narrowed and I did the only thing I could think of to disarm him—I cried.

They were genuine tears. How naive had I been to think I'd fallen off Gray's radar? And now he knew that Rabbit was his son. Moving might have saved us that—and all the decisions I did or didn't make for the past seven years washed over me, wracking sobs from my chest.

"I'm sorry," he said, making an indeterminate gesture of apology between us before walking back the other way.

I kept crying until I couldn't anymore, rolled up my window, and drove home.

THIS MORNING I'd managed to dodge my mother's pointed stares as I got Rabbit out the door—I knew I wouldn't be so lucky when I got back, and I was right, her scooter was stationed in the entry way, all the better to catch me when I returned.

"Everything okay?" she asked, taking in my haggard look.

"Yeah." I pulled off the sweat shirt—my mother had already seen, and disapproved of, all my tattoos. I had to pull myself together, flat iron my hair, and get some eyeliner on. If it were only me tattooing, freelancing like I used to, I wouldn't care, but as a boss I had to project a certain amount of authority. Especially today— after the shop being vandalized last night—my people needed me to be strong.

My mother's expression continued to be quizzical. "So—late night?"

I sighed. I hadn't told her about Dark Ink's window, I didn't want her to worry, I'd made her worry enough already in her life. "Yeah."

"Good late? Or bad late?" She looked me up and down.

"Good late. Kind of," I said, dodging around her to jog upstairs and turn the flat iron on.

"What's that mean?" she shouted up.

"It means I'm busy, mom," I shouted back, pulling on dark jeans and a red scoop-neck tee. I washed my face and smeared streaks of concealer under my tired eyes, I was going to need it today. When I walked back down stairs looking pulled together her scooter hadn't budged an inch, and now her arms were crossed.

"I just want to know when we're going to meet him is all."

"I don't know," I said, truthfully. "It hasn't been the right time." And it might never be the right time. I'd watched Mark drop fifty thousand dollars on a poker game the prior night—no matter how good we were at fucking one another, he was entirely out of my league. Not to mention the fact that he didn't know anything about Gray....

"It's just that I can see you talking yourself out of this one."

"Mom," I complained.

"No, you do this, Angie—you find a nice guy, decide he's too nice for you, and then dump him." Her words hurt like she was repeatedly running her scooter into my shin. "If I could afford to send you to some kind of counseling, I would." She revved her scooter closer and reached up to pat my cheek softly. "You're a good girl, Angela. You deserve some happiness."

I did. I knew I did—but—I forced a smile for her sake. "Thanks, Mom," I said, and leaned down to kiss her forehead. "I have to get to work," I said and whirled for the door.

"Stay out of the prisons and the pool halls!" she shouted after me, like she always did.

Good thing she didn't know I'd already been to prison once today.

I drove to Dark Ink and fought the urge to thumb through my phone for window shops at every red light. I knew Mattie would have the parlor cleaned by now—hopefully it wasn't completely freezing with just taped tarp where the window'd been—how expensive would just a plain window be? We could paint the "Dark Ink" and "24/7" on it ourselves, later, everyone I employed was an artist, including me. But every minute the shop was too cold to work in—or looked too trashy—was more walk-in clientele we'd miss. It didn't matter so much for me and the other established artists, but the new kids needed cash from flash to stay alive.

I pulled up in back, hopped out of my car, and ran around, remembering to change to a more boss-like stroll just in time to see a completely new window where the old one had been.

Our name was even bigger on this one—as was the claim that we were Vegas's only "All-Nite Tattoo", in tasteful silver cursive below.

I walked up to the window and stared at it, afraid to touch what must be very fresh paint. Inside Mattie saw me, and started waving.

As if in a dream, I walked over and through the door. Two artists had active guns, one was doing a consult, and I heard the muffled yelp of someone being pierced in back.

"Nice work, boss!" Mattie shouted, the second I was through. He pulled his hand out of its glove and brought it up to his lips for a wolf whistle. The other artists looked up, saw me, and whooped or shouted.

Mattie said something to his client, then dismounted the chair he sat on, and started patting the pockets on his leather vest as he came over. "They installed it this morning, and left this for you," he said, handing me an envelope.

I took it from him, feeling the blood drain from my face. *Another letter.* I didn't dare open it on the parlor floor.

"That's, uh, good thing, right?"

I ran a hand through my hair. "Yeah. Of course." Unless it'd been bought with Pack blood-money as some sort of perverse apology or way for Gray to make me think I owe him. I folded the letter and put it in my back pocket and scanned our current clients. None of them looked rough enough to run with the Pack, but a lot could change in seven years. So I kept my chin high and walked over to my station— I'd been in such a rush yesterday, I hadn't put my inks back, and I needed to do some sketches. One of my regulars wanted a tiger on her right shoulder, and it was just about the only blank skin that she had left, it needed to flow with all the other the work she had.

Jack's station was on the way to mine. He'd left out a half-drawn picture of the rising sun. It was beautifully rendered, you could almost feel the sunlight radiating off the page, gentle smears of pink and orange. I knew on the right skin, pale enough, he wouldn't even do any outlining, he'd make it look like watercolors. Jack had some devotees due to word of mouth—Vegas was a 24/7 town, and night-shift workers didn't want to wake up early on their off days for tats —but not a lot of them, not after 3 AM. I'd offered him more lucrative daytime slots—more lucrative for us both, since I kept a slice— but he'd always rebuffed me in his devil-may-care way.

I traced a corner of the sun he'd drawn with one finger. I had pale enough skin. And I had space, right over my hip. I imagined Jack touching me with gloved hands, felt things best left quiet stir and— my eyes caught sight of a used condom in his trashcan.

Because of course there was.

I brought a hand up to rub my temple. If he was shooting porn here, I would kill him.

I made my way to my station and gave up on worrying if the Pack could see me, opening the letter as I sat down. It was a crisp sheet of official cream stationary, carefully folded. I unfolded it slowly, and for the first time in weeks got something good in the mail:

Can't wait to see you tonight.
    M

CHAPTER ELEVEN
JACK

"I'd remind you that you can stay, but I already know that you're going, aren't you," Paco shouted at me from his living room.

He'd heard the shower stop—and I came out with an amazingly plush towel around my waist. Paco's boyfriend had as excellent taste in couches and towels as he did in boyfriends.

"Yeah, sorry," I apologized. I had to go, while Paco's blood was still singing inside me. There were some things I could only do after a fresh feed.

"Yeah, I know," Paco said, with a tease.

I dried myself off and swung the towel out to him. "You missed a spot," I said, swirling my hand over my stomach, where his was still sticky with cum.

He swatted it away. "I'm waiting for the Oreos to give me strength." He'd retrieved them from where they'd landed earlier.

"You just like smelling like me."

"Like *us*," he emphasized. "Although I'm glad we didn't make it to the bedroom. I might be too tired to change the sheets. As it is...." He looked at the disarray of couch cushions behind him, "I'm going to be tipping Imelda extra tomorrow."

I grinned. "Hey, so," I began.

Before I could say another word, he jumped in. "Here it comes."

"What?"

Paco set the Oreos aside and stood, and I appreciated him anew. He'd put on forty pounds of muscle since we'd first met—he'd been a scrawny club kid, and I'd been looking for easy prey, when he'd awakened a different hunger in me I hadn't known I'd had. Over the years, Paco'd become one of Vegas's most sought after bodyguards, and now he had a long-term contract with the Fleur de Lis, Vegas's newest, classiest, casino. From here, with the tasteful lighting from above, I could see the puckered scar where a bullet had found his shoulder instead of a client's heart.

And me? I hadn't changed. At all.

"You're a proud asshole, you know that?" he told me, falling back into drill sergeant mode.

"The proudest," I said, laying claim. Proudest that I was Paco's only, ever, top. I could go either way in the right situation, but I was the only one that ever saw that man face down.

"So now that we're agreed—yeah, I'll ask my friends on the force about Bella for you. There aren't violent murders in Summerlin too often, my curiosity'll seem natural."

"Thanks, Paco. And...."

I walked out of the magician's house, holding keys to Paco's car and wearing one of the magician's long sleeved shirts.

I DROVE Paco's dark sedan to Summerlin and parked a few blocks away from Bella's house. My car was nothing but noticeable, and there was a chance its engine had woken a few people up the prior night coming and going—I didn't want anyone thinking I'd returned to the scene of the crime.

I made sure on my way in to be unseen, which was easy, Paco's willing blood had my powers flowing at full blast. The magic that made you a vampire—it was like always being lucky. Beautiful women would angle across a room to you. Dice would roll in your favor. And what you weren't already given you could most often charm.

Someone, cops or a neighbor, had tacked some wood up over where Bella's door had been. I took some solace in the fact the lock I'd set hadn't had a chance to work—the door'd been ripped off its hinges and flung aside, pressing down a square patch of clover in the yard.

I looked around again then set my fingers against the plywood they'd replaced it with and tugged. The nails unsealed from the surrounding wood. The second it was wide enough I slunk in.

I could smell the fight before I saw it, my eyes adjusting to the darker space indoors. Bella's fear, her blood—blood I'd always wanted to know, and held back from—and the scent of her attackers. Someone—*someones*, at least two of them, but they smelled the same. Grease, like from a car shop, and something else, more animal and musty.

I made careful not to touch anything, although as a vampire I didn't have fingerprints—almost like the magic that ruled us knew we were destined for lives of crime—because if there was something the police could do, I wanted them to be able to eventually do it. I only wanted to do it faster—because the punishments I could dole out were ever so much more just.

There were signs of a struggle, strewn tarot cards, shattered crystal skulls. Her laptop was gone, and I didn't know who'd taken it, the attackers or the police. And in the bedroom, where I'd fucked her less than a day ago, a massive blood stain and a sense of death.

I walked over the line she'd drawn, her ritual spell meant to trap me—and now, with Paco's blood on board, I could feel its pull. I knelt down beside it and waved my hand out and it tugged me every time. My little witch had been magical after all—just less magical than me.

So had she seen the future? Hers—and mine? My black aura, my evilness? I waved my hand across the spell one more time, then stood. There was nothing else for me here, and it was time for some magic of my own.

I GOT into Paco's car and drove out of Summerlin. Vegas wasn't that big a city and I had hours left till dawn—it was time to cruise. I drove for downtown, intent on Bella, the scent of her blood still fresh in my nostrils. If her killers were still in Las Vegas tonight, there was a good chance I'd find them.

How? By being me—and full of blood. It was some sort of psychic dowsing—the same thing that pulled innocent creatures into my path to bleed could pull other people toward me, or me to them. So I drove east on 515 and waited.

Just past downtown, I felt a tug. Like someone was pulling a string tied around my chest. I flipped my turn signal on and followed it.

The dowsing pulled me away from the strip and further out, into the endless suburbs on Vegas's other side, until it led me into a parking lot and faded. I was circled by off brand restaurants, used clothing stores, and pawn shops—and a dive bar with all sorts of motorcycles parked out front. Hogg's Heaven, with the image of a happy pig—like it used to be a BBQ joint, except now the 'hog' referred to all the bikes parked outside. I got out of Paco's car and walked in.

I was plenty used to these kind of places. But I'd borrowed a shirt for the sleeves, I didn't want to make identifying me later any easier than it was, and the magician's starched collar made me look a little stuffy. Maybe that was a good thing and I should go with the whole tourist shtick. So instead of my usual swagger, I paused at the outside of the line of motorcycles and swallowed nervously, appearing to gather my strength before I pushed through.

My nose told me this was the right place, as soon as I walked in.

The scent of a working shop and that animal undertone hovered in the air. How would I know who it belonged to? One of the people casting me glances and pretending not to, or one of the people giving me outright glares? I couldn't go around sniffing people, so I walked over to the bar, where the bartender ignored me.

I knew he could see me, I was the only person here not wearing some sort of leather, and I might've been the only person to put on deodorant. The men around me, in conversation with one another and/or their beers, ranged in age from early twenties to late fifties, but the one thing they all had in common was that they all looked muscled and angry. The few women present had the same age range as well, only they went from nubile to weatherbeaten. Sunscreen was clearly not popular among this set.

One of the younger women broke away from a crowded pool table and walked over. "Can I help you?" Paco's blood just kept on giving.

"He was on his way out," answered the bartender for me. There was an angry scar from his eye down to his neck.

I turned toward her and smiled like I'd won the lottery, letting all of my magnetism beam down. "I was actually looking for a friend. About this tall? Dark hair? Curvy?" I used my hands to show the space Bella would occupy. "I met her, and she said she comes here." I did my best to sound missed-connections, not stalkery.

A frown crinkled her face. "Yeah, um, I haven't seen anyone like that in a while now."

She was pretty by Midwestern standards, shoulder-height to me, petite all around, perky-breasts under a patterned tee, with a denim mini and low-cut cowboy boots to show off all the leg in between. There was something earthy about her though, a little too weary and a little too wise, and I knew she was lying about seeing Bella.

"You're sure?" I pressed, positively glowing at her. I saw something flicker in her eyes, some doubt or uncertainty, but then the bartender answered.

"She's sure."

"I'll have to drink her away then." I sank against the bar dramatically, playing the mortally wounded tourist. "She was the most beautiful woman I'd ever seen. Present company excluded, of course."

The girl's eyebrows rose and she laughed, turning back to the bartender. "Come on, Wade. Let him have just one beer." Wade's leather vest had a patch that said Davis on it—so clearly he and she were on a first name basis.

I came forward, wallet at the ready. "Only if I can buy one for my champion too."

She bit her bottom lip for a second. "Any of these guys here can buy me beer anytime," she said, gesturing to the surrounding men, several of whom were keeping an eye on us. "But you can only buy me one if you go to the jukebox and pick the right song."

And that...was something the blood likely wouldn't help me with. I gave her a tight smile and tried to sound at ease. "Sure. Wait right here."

I walked over to the jukebox—it was one of those electronic numbers with an infinity of songs to choose from. And unless the magician's shirt had actual magic in it—I put one arm up against the machine, and used the other to flip through the screens. I was a fan of The Black Keys. Sinister Kid felt a little too on the nose, given what I was—but I'd always loved Howlin' for You. I ran my card through, punched the numbers, and returned to find a beer of unknown origin waiting beside the woman for me. I took a sip, glad I was immortal and likely immune to whatever the bartender'd poisoned it with, and watched the girl's face as the current song faded, and Howlin' for You came on.

As the first few chords picked up, she broke into a wide grin and gave me a sly look. "Well what do you know—you found it."

I grinned back at her and then crooked a finger at the bartender as pretentiously as possible.

CHAPTER TWELVE
ANGELA

My afternoon was booked with one of my long-standing appointments: an art deco framed back piece done Waterhouse-style of a woman with long hair contemplating herself in a mirror. The woman I was tattooing used to be a showgirl, but had retired upwards into the arms of a RV-sales millionaire. This tattoo was a commitment for her—after getting this, there was almost no way she could go back to her old life. I found it ironic that someone would spend their whole lives showing people other parts of their body, only to finally decorate those parts to be privately seen.

Three hours in, and I could tell she was over it, twitching and squeaking—especially when I got to the hair spooling near the soft skin of her waist. I got to a good stopping point then asked, "Ready to call it a day?"

"Yes, please," she said, slumping into the chair. "Longest session yet?"

"Yeah," I said, spraying water and sliding it away with a towel. "We're almost there. Just a few more hours."

She dismounted the chair, a little wobbly with endorphins, into the waiting arms of her older husband. "It's gorgeous, honey. Just as gorgeous as you," he said. His sleeves were rolled up, revealing his own faded Marine tattoos. I knew better than to offer to touch them up for him. Some tattoos were best left alone.

He steadied her as I taped her up, and I couldn't help but smile at them. He came with her each session, to drive and support her, and in the mirror I could see the way she looked at him for strength when the needles hurt. They were genuinely happy.

Would I ever get to be?

"So, three hours?" the Marine said, interrupting my thoughts.

I glanced at the clock. "Precisely."

He pulled out a wad of hundreds, licked his thumb, and counted several out for me—my time, plus a tip. I tossed my gloves in the trash, then took the cash. "Thanks, as always."

"See you next month?" she said, beaming at me. She'd rebounded into the happy part post-tattoo—the primal pleasure your body took after weathering pain.

"Of course," I said, leaning in for a very gentle hug.

I GAVE my wrist a thirty minute break, paid some bills, and did boss-like stuff, which included studiously not cramping my old artists' style while keeping an eye on the newer ones. We generally had a probationary period of three months where you had to not only prove you were decent, but that you were trainable, and that you could play well with others. I'd stopped being surprised by how many artists failed long ago. I wasn't sure if it was supervision by a woman or supervision at all—a lot of artists couldn't take suggestions. And I had high standards, for customer service, quality, cleanliness, and punctuality that my artists met or exceeded all day, every day.

All of which was to say I was in charge at all times. Which was why truly telling Mark thanks but no thanks tonight should be easy, right? *Right.*

Then I saw my next client get out of her car through my nice new Mark-provided glass window.

I PICKED Rabbit up from his afterschool program and drove us home. His favorite dinner was my favorite bribe.

"Are you going out again?" he asked over a chicken stick.

I usually only went out one or two times a week, on weekends not weekdays. "Yeah. Is that okay?" If he said it wasn't, then I could call Mark and postpon—

"Can I play videogames?" His voice rose in excitement.

My shoulders sank. Betrayed by my own son and his computer. "After you do your homework."

"Did I hear someone say homework?" my mother shouted from the living room where she was watching Wheel of Fortune. "I love homework!"

The expression Rabbit made then—caught between a ridiculous grin and an eye-roll—I could tell he was reaching that age when the adults in his life wouldn't be cool anymore soon, but we weren't there yet. I laughed at him then he laughed with me, and I felt my heart stretch tight. I would do anything for him, give my life for him. There had to be some way to never tell him he was Gray's.

"You okay, Mom?" he asked, hopping out of his chair and pushing it back in.

"Yeah," I said, forcing a smile. "Go help your Grandma learn fractions. It'll be good for her brain in her old age."

"I heard that!"

He grabbed his plate and my plate and I swatted affectionately at his bottom as he ran on by.

THE ONE FRY I'd eaten floated on a sea of stomach acid as I went upstairs to my room. What do you wear when you're fairly certain you'll be breaking up with someone? I'd been a nun for Halloween a few years back, maybe I could see if it still fit. Habits seemed very forgiving. I snorted at myself and then opened up my closet doors.

What I wound up with was a swingy black shirt-dress that had a fabric belt. It was cute, but perhaps a little more churchy than date-y. I put on cute black flats, small gold hoops and soft pink lipstick, and redid my eyes a little, but not too much. Still altogether church-ish, although perhaps a stylish and fashionable one. I was pulling my coat out of the closet when the doorbell rang.

I made it through the gauntlet of my mother and son and answered the door after peeking through the peephole to make sure it was really Mark and not some biker.

Which was, in and of itself, the biggest reason I needed to break up with him. I'd have to be looking over my shoulder for the rest of my life. I couldn't condemn anyone else I loved to that torment too.

I swung the door open and plastered a smile on. "Hey Mark."

"Hey beautiful," he said. He offered me his hand and I stepped outside.

We made it down to his car silently together, him guiding me toward the passenger side.

"So it's like that, is it?" he said, looking from the dress to me with a bemused expression.

I pretended not to know what he meant. "Hmm?"

"Hmm," he hmmed back, with a bit more gravel, and swung the door to his beemer open.

WE DROVE the same path we had the night before, back to the Fleur de Lis. "I'm not dressed for that," I complained, the second I realized where we were going. I wasn't dressed for a night out here. What if we were skipping a restaurant and going to a club?

"Relax, it'll be fine."

Easy for him to say. He parked and tossed the valet his keys, again without giving his name or taking the tag, took my hand, and pulled me inside.

The floor of the casino was like a cross between a ballroom and an art gallery. Lines of slot machines stopped where baroquely carved roulette and black jack tables began. People, classy people, wearing suits and satin, milled near each of these, with drinks in their hands, talking to their friends, blowing on one another's dice.

I let Mark lead me through and take me to an elevator on the floor's far side. In typical Vegas fashion, I'd be lost for a bit now even if I wanted to leave—all casinos were built half-labyrinth.

We stepped into the elevator and it lifted us, its glass walls giving us a view of the entire place, and it seemed to keep going for an incredibly long time.

"Where are we going?"

"*Mon Toit*—my roof," he translated for me. The elevator slowed and the doors opened, proving him right.

It was a restaurant with wall to wall views of downtown. Ever since they'd bumped the legal height restrictions up, casinos had been nudging higher—and the Fleur was currently the highest one of all. I walked through the doors and towards the windows like a moth to a flame. And then I noticed that we were apparently the only people here. "What?" I whispered, in slow realization. All the tables were set, but it was just us—Mark came up behind me, and pulled a chair out at the table with the best view.

"Care to join me?" he asked. I walked over to him and sat down, letting him tuck my chair in. He took the seat on the opposite side, and as soon as we were seated, waiters appeared as if by magic, bringing glasses of water and dark red wine.

"There're some things I need to tell you, Angela. I think some of them you maybe already know—which is why you're pulling back. All I ask—all I want—is to give you context."

I swallowed. This was a turn. "Sure."

"You know how I'm a lawyer?"

I nodded and took hold of my water glass.

"Well I haven't exactly been forthright with you. And you—you never really asked any questions—so I never had to come up with answers."

It was hard to keep the confusion off my face. "Just spit it out, Mark."

"I'm head legal counsel here. And I'm kind of a big deal."

My eyebrows rose. "Big enough to close out the entire restaurant for us deal?"

He gave me a rueful grin. "Only on a weekday. Weekends, too many people use this place for marriage proposals, I wouldn't want to ruin their fun."

"So, you're a big rich lawyer. So what?" I said. "Oh—God—is this where I find out that I'm the other woman?"

He laughed. "No—no, no, no."

"Then what? Because while cash is nice and all—"

"You remember all those movies in the 90's?" he asked and gave me a hopeful look, gesturing to indicate our surroundings.

"Barely—I was pretty young," I said, as realization dawned. Before new Vegas there was old Vegas, and old Vegas'd been run by the mafia. My boyfriend was a big rich lawyer—*for the mob.*

I wasn't sure if I was going to laugh or cry or laugh-cry. I grabbed the wine glass and took a huge swig of it, then another, as Mark studied me from across the table.

My wolf—me—one of us—had unerring instincts, dammit. To find the biggest, baddest guy in the room and fall for him.

Even when I thought I wasn't—I was.

"I understand if that means that we can't be together," he said calmly, almost cool, like I was an opponent in court. He was worried I was going to still reject him, I could see him shutting down. I put the wine down instantly, reached out a hand, and he reached for it at once engulfing it in his own.

"That's not it at all," I said.

82

"Then what happened? You've been acting strange for weeks. I assumed you'd finally googled me."

I had, once, before our first actual date, like any responsible American girl. But I'd been on my phone and stopped when Mark Carrera and a lawyer photo all came up. I put my head down in my free hand. "No. I've just been dealing with my own stuff. You're not the only one with a secret identity."

"Yeah? You go around Vegas at night, solving crime?" A tentative hope bloomed around his eyes as he teased, "Are we secretly mortal enemies?"

"Not quite." How much to tell him and not sound crazy? "You know how I have a son?"

He nodded. "I know that you haven't let me meet him yet."

"His dad—well, his dad's an asshole. He's in prison. And he's recently started to contact me." *Keep it surface, keep it safe.* "He's been sending me letters. I don't want to talk to him—"

"Who is he?"

"You mean is he a friend of yours?" I said, tilting my head to the side. "Unlikely."

His eyes narrowed. "You realize anything you don't tell me now, I could just look up later? I have sources."

I took my hand from both of his. "You wouldn't, if you were the honorable and respectful man I thought walked me through that door."

He rocked back in his chair and appraised me anew. "Touché."

"I was never caught when I was running with him, so there's nothing tying my name or my son's to his. And it doesn't matter anyhow, he's serving consecutive life sentences."

"For?"

"Bad things."

"Coy girl." He gave me that look he always did when I was too challenging—like I was a horse to be tamed or a mountain to be climbed. That look always made my heart catch in my throat and me squeeze my legs together a little more tightly, but right now I forced myself to concentrate on the situation at hand. "So what does he want?"

"He wants to see his son, who doesn't know about him. I told him his dad died."

"Oh, Angela," he shook his head quickly. "You shouldn't have lied to him."

"It was better than the truth. Trust me." I picked up a fork and spun it, just as waiters reappeared bringing rustic bread and salads. "I just don't know what to do now. I backed myself into a corner—and Rabbit shouldn't have to meet such a disappointment."

"All he's doing is writing, right?"

I inhaled to try to lie, but he made a thoughtful sound. "Last night—the window."

"Yeah. To scare me."

"Did it work?"

"Rabbit and Dark Ink are all I have." I didn't realize how lonely that sounded, till the words came out, but it was true. The things that'd happened with Gray when I was younger had scarred and scared me, leaving me more comfortable with people being a boss than a friend.

"And me," Mark said, and I looked up. His dark eyes were deadly serious. "And I have friends who have friends," he said, his voice low.

I swallowed. If he was offering what I thought he was—I—that wasn't my call—Gray'd only broken a window—and Mark didn't know what Gray was besides. "No. Please no," I said, then licked my lips. "But thank you."

"You're welcome," he said, watching me intently. "And now that both our pasts are on the table, maybe we should enjoy the view."

I looked around at the empty restaurant, emptied just for me. Then I looked out at the gorgeous Vegas night, winking hotel room lights, jagged bolts of neon, the light on the Luxor pyramid beaming up to God, and then miles of coldly beautiful desert all around. When you lived here, you forgot just how special this place could be. And lastly, I looked at Mark, who was the first person I'd almost ever told about my time with Gray—and the first person who might not run away from the real story, either. Most of it. The non-werewolf part at least.

Maybe...maybe my mom was right, and I didn't have to be alone anymore.

"Shall we?" Mark said, picking up his fork.

"Nah," I said softly, and stood. I circled around the table to him as he pushed his chair back. "How good are the waitstaff here? Would you say they're polite?" I asked, coming near to him.

"Excessively." His eyes flickered over me, wondering—hoping—what would come next.

"Good," I said, swinging one leg over his lap like I was mounting a horse, holding my skirt up as I sat down, and when I was settled I took his face in my hands and I kissed him. Sweetly. Like I was kissing him for the first time. The first time I was this girl who could trust in someone.

His hands came up instantly to press me to him, holding me, his mouth fierce against mine—I didn't think I was the only one experiencing firsts tonight, surely Mark hadn't confessed exactly who he was to many other women. I moved from his mouth to nuzzle beneath his jaw to kiss his neck, and I could've sworn I felt his blood pulsing fast in his carotid as his hands rose to catch in my hair. I was still kissing him when he pulled me back.

"You're the only woman that makes me feel like this, Angie," he said, staring into my eyes. "The only."

And some scared part of me broke, a piece of my armor, shattering forever. "Mark," I whispered, reaching between us to haul his shirt up as he started unbuttoning it from the top. He kissed me then and our hands fought as we reached for my dress's belt and buttons, till it was hanging free like a robe.

I undid my bra's clasp between my breasts and let it fall open. I didn't care who saw us, the Vegas night wouldn't judge me, and the staff were paid too well to care. I rose up high enough for him to sink his hands and free himself from his slacks, heard the zipper slide open, and then felt the heat of him beneath me as I ground against him, only my underwear in the way. We played with it then, me grinding down as he thrust up, both of us knowing the thin fabric wouldn't keep him out for long. He reached his hands to one of my hips, grabbed the side of my underwear and tore it with his strong hands, before doing the same on the other side, and yanking it away —and I got the feeling that that was what he would do to anything that stood between us. Now, and forever.

I rocked over him without him inside me, just letting our mutual heat rub, the soft shaft of his cock playing against my folds till he was slick with me, as our mouths searched one another's, his hands clenched around my ass. Then slowly, inevitably, he pulled me up as he tilted his hips down, so that the head of his cock was right at the entrance of me, and he played it there, teasing me with his tip, as I made shamelessly eager sounds.

"You want me in you?" he growled in my ear. "All the way?"

I nodded helplessly. "Please," I whispered. "Now—please."

His strong arms slowly lowered me, his chest rumbling in pleasure as my pussy took him in. "That's it," he said when my legs were spread wide and I was stretched tight around him. "Right there," he said, beginning to thrust.

That's when I knew that this was going to be his ride—which was exactly what I wanted.

What was it about getting used that felt so good? I didn't know, but with Mark I didn't have to question. It didn't change how he treated me any other time but now—he knew just what I wanted when we fucked.

I wanted to feel *owned*.

"Goddamn, Angie," he muttered, using my waist as leverage to slam himself deep. I threw my head back and gave in, my moans bouncing like my breasts against him. He paused his thrusts so he could kiss them roughly, his five-o'clock shadow scraping my skin as his lips sucked my nipples into peaks. I leaned forward panting, running my fingers through his hair, grabbing hold of his shoulders, grinding myself against him. He made a low rumbling sound of appreciation that I felt as much as heard, and as his tongue licked up, running over the rose tattoos above my breasts, it changed into a possessive snarl. "You're goddamned perfect, and I'm never going to let anything happen to you."

My breath hitched. I mean...that was what I wanted...right? To feel safe? To feel possessed? After Gray I didn't think I could ever truly believe in love again, but wasn't this the next best thing?

Mark looked up at me with a burning intensity in his eyes that both scared me and turned me on. And if ever there was a human man who could stand up to Gray....

"You swear?" I asked him, not liking how my voice quavered when I asked.

He measured me then, and I wasn't sure what future he was seeing in my eyes. I could never offer someone white picket fences, that wasn't who I was, I had it written on my skin in ink. "From here on out, Angela," he said, his voice like gravel. "You're mine."

I gasped, and then before I could say anything, he kissed me.

I fell into it and into him, holding his face as he kissed me voraciously. His cock was still hard inside me, but there was something more desperate happening now—I kissed him like I needed him to breathe. He sucked my lower lip in as if to claim it and then released it slowly, raking his teeth over my skin, and I could feel my pulse pounding, at my throat, my breast, and deep inside my hips where I still held him.

He grabbed my waist again, then slid his hands down and back until they were cupping my ass. "I'm going to fuck you so hard, Angela—you'd better hang on." And before he gave me any time to do so, he started.

He used his hands to rock me against him, driving himself in and out while he rubbed my clit against his stomach. I wound my hands in the fabric of his suit jacket, ruining its lines, crying out each time the head of his cock found my spot deep inside. I kissed at his neck, and then gave up trying, because everything was narrowing down—

my feet barely touched the ground as each of his strokes bounced me.

I was trapped there, pinned on his cock, and then I started to grind, my own ass clenching and reclenching in time, giving me small strokes off of him as my hands on his shoulders helped pull. His breath caught and held, his eyes closed, his head rocked back, enjoying the way I was writhing on him, trying to get myself off. It wouldn't be long now—this—this night—had opened something primal in me long shut down. I wanted to both give myself to him and take him inside me forever.

"Get it," he commanded, coming back to life, the muscles of his chest and abs rippling beneath me. I rocked back and forth on him like a horse. I could only make a wild sound in response, I'd found just the way to ride him and I couldn't stop now. "Fucking come hard for me. Go," he growled, and I whole-body shivered in response. His hands grabbed my ass and hauled me to him. "I need to feel you come."

My breath hitched, my hands clawed, and I couldn't help myself anymore I—I—I came with a low scream, shouting his name, giving my orgasm to him.

"Yes," he growled, thrusting up, feeling me pulse around him. "Yes," he said again, this time lower, and started fucking me hard.

Dizzy from my own orgasm and satisfied, it still felt so good to have him in me, my walls thick and tight. He grabbed me bodily with one arm and kept the other at my ass and I held him helplessly. He was just using me to please him now—he wound a hand in my hair, controlling me, and behind him, through eyes blurry with endorphins, I could see Vegas sprawled out in all her glory—and all of Vegas, if it were watching, could've seen me. Being taken. Being owned.

A fresh thrill spun inside me. My wolf liked being put in her place —and so did I.

He felt it first, I don't know how, but he did. "Oh God, can you?" he grunted, without slowing down. In response I ran my hands into his hair and kissed him with a bite, grinding my clit against him again, when he raised me up sliding out, and when he set me down spreading me wide. His hands and hips were untiring and I—I let my wolf out of her cage. For one moment we were one, our powers doubled, as we both wanted the same thing—she needed this as badly as I did.

"I can," I promised him. I could feel the energy of it coursing through my body, through us, looking for a way out. Another upstroke, and I was on the brink—another downstroke and I was thrown over. "Yes!" I cried out, curling over and into him, feeling new parts of myself open up to take him deeper, my wolf and I one as we pulled him inside. "Yes, yes, yes, yes—" I screamed until the words were unintelligible.

Mark moaned low at this, feeling my pussy grasp him, then made a strangled sound as he came himself, following me. His hips wildly spasmed and it was all I could do to hold on as he bucked me. "Take it," he growled, holding me fiercely in place, and I clung to him, feeling his hard cock bob inside me as it shot its load.

I sank down as he did, me still straddling him, both of us relaxed into his chair.

"Take everything," he murmured against my neck, before I rocked back and he slid out, him only holding me again. His hands stroked sweaty hair back. "I mean it," he whispered, kissing under my ear.

I was overwhelmed. This, here, with *him*—and I'd never come like that before. I'd never come with *her* before.

Maybe my wolf didn't hate me after all.

I pulled back from him after I'd caught my breath and saw the same faraway look in his eye—I knew he was thinking about what all the things he'd said, but he wasn't running away from me. I kissed him again, gently, and then stood on shaky legs. I felt him stand behind me, and heard him re-fasten his zipper.

"I lied," he said, and I stiffened, from picking up my dress's tie.

"You did?" I asked too quickly, and inside me my wolf crouched and snarled.

His lips quirked at my response—he knew he'd set his hook in me, as deep as his cock'd been at least. Then he smiled deep and true and I could feel the—I didn't want to call it love, emanating from him—but yes. Some crazy part of my heart stretched a little, suffusing me with heat.

Yes.

"Mon Toit—the roof—the name's a lie. There's three penthouses above us with the same view." He held out a hand. "Want to see one?"

I pulled my dress on, wrapped it, and tied it without doing any buttons, taking it from staid to sensual, and then I put my hand in his. Looking up into his eyes I answered, "Absolutely."

One of his eyebrows raised and his gaze traveled over me, like he was already thinking about devouring me again, and inside of me my wolf swung her head and tail eagerly low.

"Good," he said, and pulled me toward the restaurant's door.

CHAPTER THIRTEEN
JACK

"So what's your name, Mr. Tourist?" the girl asked.

This, I couldn't lie about, seeing as it was tattooed across my knuckles. "Jack," I said, showing her. "Yours?"

"Amber," she said. She hadn't really noticed my tattoos before, I could see her trying to make them work with the rest of me, my hair slicked back with Paco's hair gel, and in his boyfriend's too crisp shirt. "What do you do, Jack?"

I picked the safest occupation, given the room. "I work in IT. Back end server maintenance. It's incredibly lonely."

She gave me a mischievous look and then nodded sympathetically. "I bet."

I measured her for a moment. She was drinking, and this was clearly her home, so she was likely over twenty-one or at least eighteen. But there was something a little too knowing about her—maybe even a little scared. And Bella had been scared too, hadn't she?

"So what do you do, Amber?" I asked.

She took a long sip of her beer before answering, "Wouldn't you like to know?" Then she rested her a cowboy boot on the rail going around the bottom of the bar, revealing a line of wolf print tattoos padding up the inside of her left thigh—the same size and spacing as the ones that'd run under Bella's breast.

"I would," I answered, and took advantage of the rising bar sounds to lean in. "Completely," I said, my voice low.

I'd meant it when I said it, and I saw her eyes start to glaze. *Dammit.* I couldn't whammy her here, not with so many people around, she'd have repercussions if she told the truth to me in public —I slid back into tourist mode fast.

"I'm so sorry that other girl and I couldn't meet up. I took a taxi out here special...." As I yammered on I saw her attention return, none the wiser. "You know how you meet someone sometimes and you think you just know?"

"Yeah," she said, and I could see her playing a memory of her own inside her mind.

"And Vegas is the kind of place—it just leads to hoping." I stared woefully into my beer.

She put a sympathetic hand on my arm. "How long are you here for?"

"Just another day."

"Work, or vacation?"

"Bit of both."

"Well hopefully you'll get the chance to see a few more sights." Her hand squeezed my arm and didn't pull away. I looked from it to her and finally everything fell into place—the youth mixed with wisdom mixed with being here in this place—she was a prostitute. Possibly off the clock here, maybe one of these fine angry gentlemen surrounding me was her runner. Vegas was full of schemes like these, even where sex work was legal. *Bella, baby, what the hell did you get yourself into?*

To find out, I looked at Amber like a drowning man looked at a life raft. "There is one thing I know I'd like to see."

"What's that?" she asked, all innocence.

I jerked my chin toward her leg, and used a tone of voice rich with promise. "That tattoo of yours. Very, very close up."

Her lips crinkled into a half-smile. "The Midnight Inn. Room seven. Gimme half an hour."

"Excellent," I said, giving her a sly nod, and put a twenty on the bar.

THE MIDNIGHT INN was on the outskirts of town, and it was the kind of hotel where questions were not asked. If you'd had to point to Vegas's seedy underbelly on a map, your finger might not wind up here, but chances were you'd be nearby. I parked Paco's sedan down the street, and then made my way to room seven like the lady'd said, ready for anything—for all I knew ten bikers'd be on the other side of the door.

But I knocked as politely as I figured an IT guy would and was pleasantly surprised when Amber opened the door, waving shyly from across the doorjamb. Public doorways were fine, and places with OPEN signs were usually okay, but private homes—or places private by the hour—still required permission.

"Can I come in?" I asked.

"Sure," she said, and the wall that'd blocked me and only me from entering lifted.

We were in a small dim room with a desk and a queen, and I took the bed, since she was sitting on the desk.

"You know what this is, right?" she asked.

"I do," I said, reaching for my wallet again. If someone was running her, then I had to pay and for all I knew whoever he—or she, it's the new millennium—was, was outside with a stopclock. If she came out too early, or without enough cash—

"Good," she said, interrupting my train of thought. "Sometimes guys really do think they've gotten this lucky." She leaned back, gesturing up and down at herself. One of her legs was on the seat of the chair and her legs were intentionally open, showing me both her tattoo and the fact that she wasn't wearing underwear. She tilted her head and smiled. "I'm mostly surprised that you're not drunk."

"Why, should I be?"

"A lot of guys need liquid courage before they look for company. Even when they know they won't be rejected."

"Maybe that's why. They're afraid of a sure thing."

"It doesn't really matter to me—I charge the same for a dick, limp or hard. I just like the hard ones more."

I gave her a wicked grin, I couldn't help myself. "I'll try not to disappoint."

She looked me up and down. "All right." She kicked the chair away and stood up, all business. "Let's start the clock. Fifteen minutes of fucking is—"

I interrupted her. "How much is it just for me to eat you out?" It was the easiest cover, gave me the best chance to see her tattoo, and it'd take enough time to be plausible for whoever was likely waiting outside. I wasn't powerful enough to maintain a whammy for fifteen minutes, and there was a good chance she'd remember what I asked her—I wanted us parting on good terms.

She looked a little taken aback. "That's...it?"

"I told you I wanted to see your tattoos up close. I meant it." I leaned over and pulled off my own cowboy boots, before sinking back on the bed.

"That's all you want?"

"Yep." I used my elbows to shove myself higher up the bed. "I'm not even going to get naked."

She stood at the bottom of the bed, dissatisfied. I wasn't the kind of IT manager she was used to, and frankly I was shit at trying to be. Time to stop pretending.

I crossed my arms behind my head and looked at her. "I'm not paying you for pouting, Amber," I said. "But I'll pay you for an hour of your time, if you pull up your skirt and cowgirl up over my face."

She inhaled, preparing to argue, then swallowed what she was going to say. "Yeah, sure, of course," she said, walking up to the head of the bed to be by my side.

She crawled onto the mattress and slowly straddled me—she was so tiny the act hitched her skirt up to her waist, and I reached for both her lightly tanned thighs. I rubbed a thumb over the trail of paw-prints—it was well done, with no blow-outs, evenly spaced, even on the delicate and too-giving skin where it was placed. But the design was far from original, there were probably a thousand girls in Vegas right now with variations on wolf print tats. Because they were free, or they ran with the wolves, or their great-great-great-great-great grandmother was a Lakota Indian. In my time tattooing, I'd heard all the reasons, and in my experience, reasons were better off ignored—I was more interested in creating art.

"Do you like it?" she asked, looking down at me. There was a moment of vulnerability there—my current strangeness had made her afraid.

"I do," I said kindly. "I like it a lot," I said, and put my hands on her ass to push her pussy towards my mouth.

When she got there, legs splayed on either side of my shoulders, I reached in to pull her thighs apart, exposing her to me. I breathed on her gently, once, twice, and then started in with the tip of my tongue, inspecting every fold, every crevice. She made noises, pretend ones I knew, like women in cheap porn, and started to writhe, reaching back a hand for my cock.

"Stop that," I warned, grabbing both her wrists and pulling straight down, making her sit atop me, then I continued.

She tried making the noises again—I wondered if there was someone outside she was performing for, listening in—and I ignored her this time. Because I could sense the blood flowing down, feel the way she was becoming more swollen, scent the heat of her wetness rolling in. My tongue played with her, played against her, I sucked here, I sucked there, only staying in one place long enough to torture her.

And the sounds she made overhead slowly became more earnest, the way her breath caught when I ground my chin up and into her pussy with its light stubble, the moans she released as I kissed her clit. Her thighs pulsed against me, wanting to ride, trying to show me more of her and I let go of her hands and grabbed for her waist to keep her near as I cupped my mouth around her clit and sucked on it like I was drawing the juices from a peach. Her breath caught again, this time off-kilter, as her thighs began to shudder. Her hands were on either side of my head, clawing into the mattress, pulling the sheets beneath me tight.

I growled into her pussy, letting the sound reverberate through her, pressed my chin higher, and then rolled my tongue over her clit, swollen and fat, again and again, her juices raining down on me.

She started with a soft scream, almost soundless, and then bucked forward hard, pounding my head into the mattress. She screamed three times after that, as her hips fucked me. I held on, kept rolling her thick clit with my tongue, kept my chin up for her grinding, until she let out one final shout and pulled away from me, kneeling over me in disarray.

"You," she said when she could breathe again. "You—should bottle that."

I kissed the inside of her thigh. "I would if I could."

She brought a hand between us and stroked my lips, slick with her. "Will you do that again? If I blow you?"

"Yes." My cock had been hard ever since her ass had landed on me. "Turn around."

Amber did as she was told, dismounting me one way, and spinning to mount me the other, setting her perfect ass on my chest. I felt her undo my belt, unzip my fly, and reach in. The second her hand wrapped my cock, I wanted to thrust. No matter what I'd done to Paco earlier in the night—the hunger was always waiting. Sometimes louder, sometimes quieter, but it was always there.

I heard her make an appreciative noise, and felt her tilt forward, as a lock of her hair fell across my balls sending a shiver up my spine. And then her little mouth opened and started kissing my cock's head. Slowly and surely she started working her mouth down my shaft. I could close my eyes and imagine her lips stretched tight, sliding down, as I felt her do so—I made an animal sound and pulled her waist back towards me. With her spread like this in front of me, it was easier to suck her, and I already knew how she liked it—I grabbed her ass with both hands, and buried my face between her legs, lapping at her clit.

She moaned, I could feel it on my cock, and she started sucking me, up and down, playing my shaft with her hand when it was out of her mouth, as she ground her hips into me, and soon there was something desperate in it, like she wasn't in control anymore. She was working my cock, I could feel it sliding home to the back of her throat with each thrust, and I grabbed her bodily, rubbing her against me, trying to eat her pussy harder and have her take even more of my cock in turns.

Then she braced up on all fours suddenly. I didn't have time to complain before she reached into the pocket of her poor twisted skirt and threw a condom at me. "Put that on."

I scrambled up, shoved my jeans lower, and slid the latex on me, pleased with the lipstick stains around my shaft, as she turned to present me her pussy.

"Fuck me," she panted, her pretty lipstick smeared.

"Of course," I said, just as rough. I grabbed her hips and pulled her toward me.

My cock slid into her in one smooth motion. She was wet as hell, and she groaned as I reached deep inside her.

After that, it was fucking. Me her, her, me, our bodies knew what they wanted to take from each other. I pulled her ass apart to land me deeper and she tossed her head, making a guttural sound, her blonde hair streaming forward and back—like Angela's. Amber had the same color hair, the same tight small body. God if only I was fucking Angela right now—my cock somehow got harder at the thought of it, of taking Angela like this, hilt deep in her hot pussy instead—and I saw Amber's hands winding in the sheets again.

"Don't stop!" she begged me.

I reached forward and grabbed hold of her hair, yanking her back on me. "Does it feel like I'm stopping?" I growled, rhythmically thrusting. "I could go all night."

She shuddered at this, and I felt her pussy start to quiver around me—I let go of her hair and grabbed her hips again, pounding myself in—if she was going to go I needed to go with her.

"God—oh—God—oh—ohhh!" her last word became something wild, as I brought her onto me and held her there, burying myself inside her, conscious of my own need for release. One long stroke, two long strokes, three—swording myself through her spasming pussy, feeling the life from her flow into me—I exhaled roughly as cum shot out of me in a rush, and my own hips bucked, shoving it deep into her. When I slowed, she buckled forward with a final moan, and I slid out.

"What the fuck," she whispered to herself, not a question. I stepped off the bed and walked to the bathroom, looked for a trash can, found one, and saw that my condom was not the first of the night. "What the everliving fuck," she said louder, as I walked back in the room.

"That's kind of my thing," I said. I pushed my cock back in my jeans and zipped up. After this session, everything on me needed to be laundered, and I might still have to explain to Paco why his lovely black sedan smelled like pussy and balls.

She rolled over and pushed herself up on her elbows as I came near, but still hadn't pushed down her skirt. "So that tattoo—what's it mean?" I asked.

Her orgasmically pleased face smiled slowly. "Property of the Pack."

The Pack? The notorious biker gang? I didn't know them, but I knew of them, everyone even tangentially related to Vegas's under-belly did. Why would they've been interested in Bella—or her, them?

I sat back down on the edge of the bed and tried to play off my silence. "You're sure that's what it means? Not return to sender? Or a sell-by date?"

Amber shoved her skirt down with a snort. "You're so funny."

"Yeah, sometimes I get that, too." I pulled out my wallet and handed over several hundred and a few twenties. That was about the going rate for services on this side of town, plus a decent tip. People who worked in customer service had to have one another's backs. "Think if I could stay another night, there'd be any way I could run into that dark haired chick again?"

She rolled on her stomach toward me to take my cash. "I don't know. I haven't seen her around for the past week or two. I think she pissed someone off and is laying low."

"Pissed off who?" I said, leaning in, bringing all the force of Paco's blood behind it. Her eyes glazed for a moment, but I probably didn't even need my whammy after the way I'd fucked her.

"I don't know. One of the big guys. Wade, Murphy, Daziel, or Jonah. But I don't know which one." Damn. She blinked and shrugged as my whammy faded. I rocked back up, I had to return the car and the shirt before I crawled into bed.

"Oh well," I said, like her answer hadn't mattered to me. "Thanks for the entertainment." I walked to the door.

"You are more than welcome," she said with a smile. "You know, when you said that...I almost believed you."

I paused with the door open. "Which part?"

"The all night part."

"Too bad my hour's up. Guess we'll never know." I gave her a wolfish grin, and then closed the door behind me.

CHAPTER FOURTEEN
ANGELA

I watched the Fleur de Lis shrink as my driver pulled away. I'd almost spent the night there. The penthouse Mark'd taken me to —if anything had cemented the Cinderellaness of the evening, it'd been rolling around in 800 thread count sheets. But at 5 AM I'd made Mark let me leave him there, and he'd called a driver for me, they were outside the hotel's roundabout the second the doorman opened the lobby's door.

I had to be home and showered before Rabbit got up so I could take him to school. He knew I went out at night sometimes, but I wanted him to feel like he was most important, because he was.

And Mark...might actually get to meet him. That silly hopeful ache inside my chest got bigger.

I unlocked the door carefully and crept in, past my mother's snores. My room had its own bathroom, thank God, so I was showered, bright-eyed and bushy-tailed by dawn, rousting Rabbit for his own shower. I didn't feel nearly as tired as I had the prior night— why? Mark?

No. *Her.* I looked down at my chest like there was a way I could see my wolf surging underneath my skin. She was close—close enough to give me her strength. If only I could trust her there. I reached for the cabinet over the coffee maker and pulled out my colloidal silver with its eyedropper.

Could I risk it? I liked feeling like this—powerful and present, ready to take on anything. I could see why the Pack worshipped it—this had to be more potent than any drug.

But my wolf was at heart an animal. She operated by different rules, ones I didn't understand. And as long as I was operating in the world of mortal humans, I couldn't take that chance—I closed my eyes and swallowed an eyedropper full of silver, feeling it sizzle on my tongue. Exhaustion came up almost instantly, as my wolf sank back and my frail body won. *Damn.* I went back upstairs to put more concealer on. I heard Rabbit's shower cut out and him start singing the theme song to a video game he liked in Japanese.

And then someone rang the doorbell and pounded on the door.

Rabbit reached the stairs first, racing down ahead of me. "Hold up!" I shouted, as he went for the door. "What'd I tell you?"

Consternation furrowed his little face. "That only grown-ups can answer the door."

"That's right," I said, shooing him away with one hand. I peeked out the peephole and didn't see anything.

Had Mark sent flowers? I wasn't the only one falling—I knew it.

Then I heard a motorcycle start up. Oh no. First Dark Ink—now my apartment? I leaned against the door till the bike was gone.

"Mommy?" Rabbit asked, sensing my fear.

I crouched down. "Shh. Go back and wake up Grandma."

He didn't want to, but he also didn't want to disobey. Rabbit went down the hall as slowly as possible, looking back every chance he could. When he'd turned the corner, I opened the door.

There was nothing outside but a long box. I looked both ways down the hall before picking it up—there was something heavy inside, I could feel it rocking. With great reluctance, I took off the lid.

There was an unsigned note that read:

I still love you.
I mean it.

Over what I was very sure was Wade Davis's severed cock.

I stumbled back inside and put it in my freezer where my mother couldn't reach, as Rabbit tumbled back down the stairs. "Who was it? Grandma's up!"

"It was nothing, sweetheart. An accident," I said. But I knew the second I dropped Rabbit off at school, I was going to have to call Mark.

CHAPTER FIFTEEN
JACK

After my night out I had a lead, but I didn't have answers. *What could Bella have wanted with members of the Pack?*

I drove away from Paco's house—I hadn't gone inside to be tempted. His place was isolated, so I left his keys under his doormat and the magician's shirt inside the car with a note that said, "Wash me," as if the smell of sex on it wasn't warning enough.

Playing with the Pack didn't seem like Bella. She'd always seemed too smart for that, she didn't need drugs to get high, she saw enough strange things without them. Maybe the Pack'd promised her a lead on ayahuasca. I snorted, and took my Lincoln on the exit toward my apartment. I wanted to dowse again, to see where the blood would lead, but it was too close to dawn. Hopefully I'd still feel Paco's blood tomorrow.

It wasn't until I pulled into my parking spot that I looked at my phone. A short note from Paco, sent two hours after I'd left, I must've missed it with all the fucking. *Check ur email*, was all it said, and I rushed inside.

Sugar was excited to see me, talking at me in Siamese. I picked her up to pet her and went for my desk. I did most of my drawing at

Dark Ink on the nice drafting table, but I had a small set up here that included paints and a computer. I didn't have much cause to look at porn anymore now that I was living my so-called-life, but I still kept it connected to the internet, mostly to scan my art in. I logged in and checked my email, and sure enough Paco'd sent me one, no message, just with a few attachments.

Crime scene photos. He did have the hook-up, after all, even after midnight. I downloaded them one by one, watching the last images of Bella resolve, and flipped through them slowly, looking for something, I didn't know what. I stayed on the last one, her face vacant, dark hair spilled across the carpet, like a mirror of her blood.

There had to be a reason she overlapped with the Pack—and they didn't seem like the type who wanted their palms read. I worried at it as long as I could, looking for something in the photos I hadn't seen already in person, finding nothing. It was almost dawn when I emailed Paco back.

Thanks.
What've you got on the Pack?

I let the cursor blink there for a moment and added: *(also really make sure you wash that shirt)* and hit send.

After that I took a long hot shower and crawled in between the wooden walls of my bed-fortress, pulling the lid on before dawn rose.

I woke up the same way I'd died, with Sugar scratching outside my coffin. "Hey," I reassured her, and went for my computer.

Paco'd come through again. *Shirt's clean, but from the smell of it, you'll never be able to wash the stain off your soul.*

Here's what you wanted—let me know why. The Pack's bad news. Don't mess with them. I mean it.

This time the attachments were even more extensive.

A lot of them were things I'd heard already, bikers, guns, drugs, and a lot of interesting suppositions—mysterious disappearances they weren't able to tie to the club due to missing bodies. Of course a member of the Pack would run girls.

But why would Bella let herself be run?

I searched the documents for the names Amber'd given me, Wade, Murphy, Jonah, Daziel and all of them had been in and out of jail, manslaughter, smuggling, lighter charges. The only one who'd ever gotten caught truly red handed was their leader, Gray, and he was 'safe' in prison, protected by Las Vegas's PD.

I rocked back from the desk and wiped my face—it was only nine PM, and I didn't have much more to go on than I did twelve hours ago. I was going to have to go back to that bar, but I could guarantee nothing nefarious was going to happen there before midnight.

Sugar meowed up at me.

"Yeah, you think so?" I asked her, reaching down to knuckle her head. "I agree. It's time for laundry."

I gathered up the things I'd been wearing for my past few encounters and came up with a pile of worn-in dark denim and soft cotton t-shirts, put on some of the same, and walked down the hall with a fistful of quarters.

Paco's blood and sex had muted my hunger to a dull roar, like quiet TV-static heard through a closed door, but it was still there. It never went away. Today I'd be fine, but tomorrow I'd have to go searching or hope to get lucky. I shoved everything into a washer, fed the machine, and waited till I heard it start just in case, as another tenant walked in, walking to a finishing dryer.

I gave him a companionable smile and a nod, and caught him staring. My arms were visible and my tattoos made a lot of people stare. His stare went a bit past that though, pushing into the territory of being checked out.

So I returned the favor. He was a little younger than I looked, toned and blonde. His shirt advertised a yoga shop in Florida, where I believed he was from, given his thorough tan.

"You new here?" I asked him.

"Yeah. Just moved in. Fourth floor, back corner."

I replied with a slightly more coy, "Nearby," and a jerked chin towards the rest of the apartment complex. "How do you like it so far?"

He looked to the ceiling for a moment, then laughed. "It's less humid than Florida was. But I don't know many people yet—and my job—all I do is move cars from one lot to another when a radio tells me to. I don't meet other drivers, much less other people."

You only told stuff like that to strangers when you wanted a friend. "Yeah." I leaned back, feeling the running washer churn against me. "It's even worse to be lonely when it seems like everyone else is having fun."

"Exactly," he said, nodding hard. He looked at me a moment too long, and then nervously looked away. He was interested. I was interested. Under his attention my hunger had perked up its ears and trotted over. But this was my own apartment complex—and I could make it a day without sex.

I rocked forward. "Try Bastille. Or the Phoenix. You'll make friends in no time."

His face flushed a little and he looked down. "Thanks."

"You're welcome," I said, and tried not to graze him as I left, which was hard when the room was so small, but I managed, walking back to my apartment with an inconvenient hard on.

I did more research on the Pack on my own, and tried to figure out tonight's plan. I'd seen what Wade looked like last night—I'd cruise through the bar, make sure he was there, and then stalk him. Once I got him alone, I'd make him fess up, and then the punishing would begin. I stretched out the fingers of my right hand then pulled them into a fist, making a satisfying crunch.

The timer I'd set on my phone rang and I walked back down the hall. Just thinking about drinking blood again made me hungry. Paco's blood was excellent, but there was something to be said for the blood of a complete stranger, with their frightened adrenaline still singing inside.

Then I turned the corner into the laundry and found Florida standing there.

"Hey," he said, looking sheepish.

"Hey," I responded. He wanted my attention—now he had it.

"I, uh, saw the setting on your washer. I knew when you'd be back."

I tilted my head to hide a smirk. "You lay in wait for guys often?"

"Only when they look like you." He dared to meet my gaze. I stood still, considering. I'd been thinking about blood all the long walk down here and I'd had to fight down my earlier hard on. But this place was where I slept—where I died. I needed to keep it safe. Even if I could scent the sharp hopeful smell of precum in the air—and knew that he'd been thinking about me for the past hour, too. "I'm sorry," he began, taking my silence the wrong way. "I shouldn't have—"

"I don't mind," I said quickly. I didn't want my reluctance to possibly chase him back into a closet. "But—"

"You have a boyfriend."

"No." It wasn't too late—and everything about him reminded me of the sun that I'd lost, the way his skin shone, the blonde streaks in his hair. It made me want to do things to him, mad things, wild things, to see if I could take the sun from him and pull it into me. And as if sensing my wavering resolve, he stepped closer. "I have plans," I said.

"I could be fast," he promised.

Then the door swung open behind me, revealing Mercy, the pregnant woman who lived three doors down. "Evening boys!" she announced, carrying her laundry basket in front of her belly before setting it down nearby.

"Hey Mercy," I said, then gave Florida an enigmatic smile before turning to the task at hand. When I was done tossing my clothes into the dryer, he wasn't there.

JUST AS WELL, I thought, setting back down the hall. I had things I needed to do tonight—to concentrate on. It wasn't every day you set out to kill a man on purpose. It ought to require some thought.

But by the time I got back to my apartment my cock was practically chafing and my attention divided.

Goddammit, Florida.

I locked the door behind me, paused to consider my options, and then reached for the buckle of my belt. If I'd said yes to him—and if Mercy hadn't interrupted—how would things have gone down? I pushed my jeans down, freeing myself—I wasn't going to get any other action tonight, and satisfying myself did nothing to keep the hunger at bay—but if I wanted a clear mind, nothing'd get me there faster.

Of course I knew how to play myself—no one knew better than I did what my cock liked. I stood in my entry way, one hand out to balance against the wall while the other stroked my shaft, imagining my cock sliding in and out of Florida's tan hand—or if we'd blocked the doors with our bodies and jacked each other off instead—or better yet, if he'd knelt down to suck on me while I stroked my hands through his blonde hair and brought his mouth harder, deeper, onto me—I shivered, making myself rock hard. Touching myself felt good, touching myself while imagining the depraved things I could've done to him—like sliding my cock into that yoga-toned ass of his—was even better.

I wrapped my fingers looser but stroked more quickly, imagining if I'd pinned him up against a wall, the sound of the washers and dryers covering his rising moans, me slapping his hands away from his own cock as I reached around to grab it instead, and in my mind I heard him give a satisfied grunt each time my balls slapped him as his ass took me deep and—I rose up on the balls of my feet and leaned forward, hips thrusting as I let out a low moan, as I spilled myself out into my hand.

I waited until I was done, breathing hard but feeling infinitely more relaxed. "Are we done now?" I asked my cock with a head-shake, and went to the bathroom to wash my hands, mind finally clear enough to contemplate murder.

CHAPTER SIXTEEN
ANGELA

Nine a.m. found me sitting in the very tastefully appointed waiting room of Carrera Law with a thawing severed penis in a box in my tote bag.

I'd somehow managed to get Rabbit to school and then go back home and dress up like it was just another day at work, giving my mother a cheerful good-bye on my way out the door with a detour past the freezer on my way, like I was taking a burrito for lunch and not a body part.

"I need to see Mark, is he in yet?"

The receptionist had told me he wasn't, and she wasn't sure when he would be—I told her to call him for me, to tell him I was here.

I could've called him myself—but it was the kind of thing I needed to explain in person. I needed to see his eyes when I told him about the Pack. After the way we'd fucked last night—I needed to believe. So I'd told Mattie to rebook all my appointments for today, and settled down into an overstuffed armchair for the duration.

It was hard to ignore that I was carrying a fucking body part. Literally. The same dick that'd—my jaw clenched. I'd been the one who'd signed Wade's death warrant by telling Gray what he'd done to me. But him doing that? Had been all him. I found it hard to muster much sympathy.

"Angela?"

Mark pushed in the doors looking worried and my heart leapt in my chest as I jumped out of my chair and flew across the room to him. He held his arms open just in time for me to run into them. I hadn't realized how close I'd been to crying till just then, but now that I was safe I bit my lips to stop from sobbing.

"Baby, what happened?" He put his hand under my chin and pulled my head up. I looked around—we were making a scene—I was making a scene—

"Can we go into your office?"

"Of course," he said, politely detaching himself to lead the way. I grabbed my bag and followed closely.

MARK SAT on the opposite side of his desk from me, though I'd hauled my chair far closer than any client ought to. The box was sitting between us, as yet unopened.

"I was younger then, okay?" I gave up and told him all about my time with the Pack, and his eyes had widened and narrowed at the appropriate parts of the story. "And—I got Rabbit out of it. So it wasn't all for nothing, you know?" There was a pile of used tissue in my lap—I'd spent half of the last hour crying.

"I know," he said. I saw the muscles in his jaw clench and I winced inside. A lot of guys didn't want to know who you'd been with prior—what if now he thought less of me? "I have to say—apart from all the times Gray was an asshole to you—I like his style."

My head reared back. "What?"

"If I found out anyone raped you, I'd cut their dick off too." He nudged the box with a finger. "May I?"

"Sure," I said, curling up in a ball in the chair, tissues falling to the ground.

He sidled one end of the box open and looked in. "That is, indeed, a severed penis."

"Yeah." I held my head with both hands. "Mark, what do I do?"

"You could go to the police."

"You say that like there's another option."

He tilted his head and stared at me. "You wouldn't be here if there wasn't."

He was right. There was a reason I hadn't called the cops earlier. I didn't believe they could protect me—but more importantly—"I don't want Rabbit to know who his father is."

"And now I get why."

I nodded helplessly. "I can't believe I'm here, asking you for help —I never wanted to be the damsel in distress. I've spent so long rebuilding my life into something I can be proud of—but I don't know what else to do."

Mark reached out and pulled the box across the desk to him. "I'll handle it." He opened a lower desk drawer and set the box inside.

"But Gray—"

"Is in an eight by eight cell. You matter to him, the note says so. He won't do anything to hurt you or Rabbit."

"For how long?"

"Long enough."

"For?" I asked, unable to help myself.

"If there's ways of getting messages out of prison—there's ways of getting messages in. Very clear ones."

I bit my lips hard before asking, "Do I want to know what they'll say? Or how they'll be delivered?"

He shook his head slowly. "You do not."

I nodded softly. Gray was tough—but vulnerable. He was taking silver, just like I was—and I knew he wasn't immortal—I knew Pack members could die—but he'd haunted Rabbit and I for so long

—

Mark stood and rounded the desk to me. "It's going to be okay, Angela."

I looked up at him, fresh tears welling in my eyes and the flutter of panic in my throat. "How can you be so sure?"

He went to his knees beside me. "This is what I do." He took my head in his hands and kissed the teardrops from my eyes. It was such a gentle thing to do it stunned me, and when he pulled back and I opened them, he was staring right at me. "I'll never let anyone hurt you again."

And for the first time, in my entire post-Gray life, I believed. I leaned forward and kissed him desperately. He resisted for a second, then kissed me back just as hard—harder even, his tongue pressing me back into the chair with the weight of him close behind. And as he leaned over me a heavy weight fell into my hips and my pussy ached—*Oh-God-yes-please-this-again-now-here*—and deep inside my wolf howled.

Then he pulled back. "Angela—we shouldn't." I must've looked stricken because he took my hand down the front of him to where his hard cock sat inside his suit slacks. "I do want you—I want to keep you here all day."

"Good, because I want to stay," I said, stroking him eagerly. "Mark—you make me feel safe. You don't know how long it's been," I confessed.

His expression warmed—but he started shaking his head. "You have to go—you need to pretend to be living your life normally. They can't know anything's changed."

"I wasn't followed on my way here." I'd been smart enough to check. "I was careful." He swallowed, his chest beginning to rise, and I could see him torn between his duty and his need. "Make it fast. Make it hard," I pleaded—and he reached for his belt buckle with a growl as I hitched up my skirt.

I barely had it above my waist when he took my ankles and hoisted them high, setting one on each shoulder, and then he was on me, pulling my panties aside to push himself in. He slid in all the way to his hilt, and I felt myself stretching deliciously around him—and then he started to pound, taking me at my word, no time for tease or build up, just the ferocity of desperate fucking, when one person needed to give and the other needed to be filled.

I bit my lips to hold back the sounds I wanted to make, the small cries of surprise, the satisfied moans of pleasure—*he wanted me*—after everything I'd told him he still wanted me—*wanted to be with me*—wanted to be so deep inside. His hands were holding the chair over my head, and I was curled into a comma, it was all I could do to hold on. But I didn't even need to come—I just needed to feel him inside me—then one of his hands snaked between us and he started to play with my clit with his thumb.

"Mark—" I protested in a loud hiss.

He chuckled, but he wouldn't stop—he redoubled his efforts, until his pounding was a steady rock and his thumb kept rubbing till it found the right spot which he knew when I kicked up against him, trying to get more of his thumb as he fucked me.

My eyes closed and my toes pointed and my whole body tensed until I came for him, biting on my own hand to stop from screaming.

He, however, had no such compunction. "Angela," he growled, and I felt his cock stiffen inside me, ready to fill me with its load. "Angela—baby—Angela," he shouted, his hips spasming against mine, his cum pouring out, so much I would've sworn I could feel its heat pooling inside.

He collapsed over me, breathing hard. We'd only taken less than five minutes, I knew, and yet I felt like I'd been safe for hours. Mark hauled himself up to kiss me. "How can you do that to me, every time?" He pulled back, sliding out, taking a tissue off the desk to clean himself.

I lowered my legs more slowly. I loved being filled—I didn't want to lose the sensation. "Won't you get into trouble?" I was already wondering what kind of walk of shame I'd have to do outside. Mark's office had windows. All the blinds were pulled, but there was no way a secretary hadn't heard.

He smiled and rose back up onto his feet, setting himself inside his slacks again. "It's called Carrera Law for a reason. Also the walls are sound proof."

"And you didn't tell me?" I protested, standing up to set my skirt back down. My panties were too thin a barrier to protect my skirt from his cum—I'd have to change clothes the second I got home.

"It was too hot watching you try to be quiet. Which you weren't, by the way, but the trying made me harder."

I flushed. "I'd have thought that was impossible."

"Then wait till the next time you're in here, when you're bent over my desk and I'm taking your ass on it."

My thighs pulsed together at the thought of it and warm things inside me sank. "Goddamn you, Mark."

He laughed and leaned forward to kiss me, far more chaste than anything that'd come before. "I want you thinking about that all day, Angela. None of your other problems, you hear me? The second you start to worry, I want you to start thinking about me taking your ass and filling it with my cock."

I wanted to tell him that was impossible, that the things I had to fear were far greater than the primal urge I felt when we were together. But right now, half-panting, with his cum leaking out and slicking my thighs, I genuinely couldn't.

"Okay," I whispered.

"Good," he said, and grabbed my ass hard enough to help me imagine. "Go home, have a normal day, and I'll talk to you tonight."

I leaned up on my toes to kiss him, then picked up my much lighter bag.

CHAPTER SEVENTEEN
JACK

I parked my vintage Lincoln Continental down the street from the Hogg's Heaven, far enough that no one would associate me with my car, and walked in.

My hair was done differently tonight, as were my clothes and my attitude. I wore my black cowboy boots, my darkest jeans and a black t-shirt under a leather jacket that was form fitting, utilitarian, not ostentatious. I scanned the bikes for clues, but members of the Pack weren't fond of personalized plates, so I walked in.

Amber wasn't there, which was a good thing. But neither was my mark for the evening, Wade—one of the other members was behind the bar. I bellied up, well aware of the stink-eye I was getting, and leaned over when the bartender came to tell me to go.

"I have a business proposition for Murphy—is he here?" I picked another of the Pack's leaders at random, pushing my remaining blood-luck.

One of his furry eyebrows rose, disbelieving me. "Tell me and I'll tell him."

I shook my head. "My boss said only me—and only in person."

"Your boss being?"

Who was the scummiest currently? Vegas had a lot of churn, it was hard to keep up. "Jayson. From New York." I'd done a tattoo on one of his underlings recently, who'd talked up his boss's dark side, and I'd smelled the gun oil on him.

The bartender measured me, as did the men in earshot on either side. "And the business?"

I pretended to be bored. "Import, export. Your sort of thing. I'll tell Murphy the specifics."

He wanted with all that was in him to blow me off, but instead he went into the back. After a few minutes he returned, smelling like a Cuban cigar.

"Murphy says after the last time, your boss can go fuck himself—and you're lucky that we don't fuck you."

I leaned in to protest. "Come on, I can't go back to Jayson with that—"

The man to the side of me pulled out a knife and planted it into the wood between us. "You do, or you don't go back at all."

I looked from him to the bartender, and pushed back in the way I thought a petulant criminal underling might, then walked outside. I had what I needed—Murphy was here.

Under the streetlight outside a group of bikers were talking shop, holding beers in one hand and cigarettes in the other. You could still smoke inside in Vegas, especially at a place like this—but a lot of places had smoking pavilions out back, where one could shoot the shit in a civilized fashion, smoking beneath the stars. I walked down the street and then pulled left, coming up behind the rest of the strip mall. After a cursory glance to make sure I wasn't seen, I jumped up and caught the edge of the GOLD 4 CASH's awning and pulled myself up.

The strip mall's roof was sun battered, with a few scattered tarps held down by rocks to keep intermittent rains at bay. I kept low and near the center where anyone on either side would be hard pressed to see me, until I knew I was over Hogg's. Then I crept towards the back and was rewarded with a plume of cigar smoke. *Murphy.* I smiled cruelly and leaned over to sight him.

He was a stocky red-haired bearded man—looked almost like a dwarf from one of those fantasy movies—and he was pacing in a small circle, clearly agitated, listening to someone on his phone without answering except to say, "Yes. Yes."

When he was done he pocketed it and turned to someone under the awning where I couldn't see.

"You've gotta calm down, Murph."

"Easy for you to say—you didn't have to do it."

"You could've said no."

Murphy stopped pacing. "Don't pretend that—"

"You've got free will—"

"Fuck you, Daziel. You know the plan."

"Yeah. And Wade was in on the plan until Gray changed his mind."

"He's in there because of us. I'm not turning my back on him."

"I wouldn't either."

There was the soft sandy sound of a cigarette being quenched and the other speaker emerged. Daziel was long and lean and rugged, everything about him looked well-worn, from the bends in his boots to his shaggy salt and pepper hair. Well-worn in a prepared way—and another of the 'big-dogs', according to Amber.

Murphy came over and jabbed a finger up at him. "You picked a hell of a night to be out of pocket."

"Sorry for wanting to find someone a little taller to blow me."

"Goddammit, Wade's dead, stop joking."

"Joking's how I cope, brother. Always." He fished in his vest and pulled out a fresh cigarette. "I don't envy what you and the others had to do. Glad I missed it, honestly."

I inhaled the secondhand smoke deeply, contemplating. I could jump down there and kill them both easily. I had otherworldly strength. But I couldn't torture and bleed one effectively without killing the other and there was always the chance that I'd kill the wrong one first....

"And all over that whore. I can't believe her pussy's worth more than Wade's life."

My ears perked. That whore—did they mean Bella?

"It ain't the whore. It's the kid."

"Then we take the kid." Murphy said, pounding a fist into an open hand.

"But he don't want it like that," Daziel said.

Murphy grunted. "Too much silver's made him soft." He reached into his vest and lit another cigar and went through the ritual of clipping it, lighting it, sucking the smoke deep. "I did the right thing, didn't I?" he asked, after exhaling the first fragrant puff.

Daziel did a whole-body shrug. "You did what Gray wanted. That's close enough."

I rocked back on the roof. Now that I knew what they looked like, retribution was just a matter of time.

CHAPTER EIGHTEEN
ANGELA

Somehow, all day long, I managed to do what Mark'd told me to. I went home and showered, dodging my mother's requests, and had Mattie salvage one of my appointments for the afternoon, blaming car trouble, which with my car was all too likely. Then I picked up Rabbit, went to the grocery store, got everything for dinner, and went home to start cooking like nothing had changed.

Any time my mind wandered, I remembered Mark's promise and the way his hand had clenched me. Like I was his.

Only I'd been clenched like that before—by the man who was haunting me now—

"Mom?" Rabbit asked, looking up from his coloring book on the dining room table. "Where's my red crayon?"

"I don't know, sweetie. Can you use another color?"

"It's Santa mom. He's mostly red—"

I tasted the marinara sauce I was heating. It needed salt. "Try pink. Or blue. Or green. Santa's only limited by your imagination."

Rabbit shook all his crayons out so he could search them. "You wouldn't want me to color a firetruck yellow would you?"

"Of course not. That's silly," I said, making a face so he'd know I was teasing. "Also firetrucks are real."

Unlike Santa—but like werewolves.

The doorbell rang and Rabbit sprinted for it—but I got there just in time, catching his shoulders and spinning him around to face me. "What've I told you about opening the door?"

"Don't do it, ever."

"Ever, ever," I said, staring straight into his eyes.

"Mom, you're hurting me," he said, trying to shrug away.

"Ever," I repeated, pushing him back. I leaned up to the peephole —and saw Mark. I reached for the door and pulled it slightly open. "I —thought you were going to call."

"I decided to visit instead," he said, holding up a bottle of wine, and a bouquet of flowers. "Can I come in?"

And I realized he was asking to come inside. He'd always gathered me up from here before, respecting the boundary I'd kept between my dating life and my home, we'd always stayed out, or over at his condo. But I'd never spent a full night away from home— and I'd never let him in.

Until now. I stepped back, making room, giving him a tentative smile. "Sure. Do you like spaghetti?"

He gave me a look, one eyebrow rising. "I'm Italian."

I laughed. "Perfect."

I heard the whine of the scooter's electric motor as my mother pulled in. "Is this Mark?" she asked pointedly, looking between the two of us.

"Yes, Ma'am." Mark strode over and held his hand out. She shook it warmly.

"Nice to finally meet you! Please, take off your coat, make yourself at home." He grinned and slipped his jacket off, putting it on the back of a nearby chair. I noticed he was wearing a different suit than he'd worn this morning. At least I wasn't the only one a little put out by our rendezvous.

"Mom?" Rabbit asked from the other room, peeking around the wall. Brave when the door was closed, not so brave with it open.

"Rabbit, this is Mark. Mark, this is Rabbit."

True to his namesake, Rabbit came out warily, his blonde hair tousled every which way.

"Nice to meet you, Rabbit," Mark said, with his sonorous voice, and held out his hand.

Rabbit sized him up and then took it, shaking it like he must've seen on TV.

"That's a good shake there."

"Thanks. Who are you?"

I bit my lips to keep from laughing, as Mark looked over at me. "I'm, uh, one of your mother's friends."

"Oh—okay," he said, then dodged around Mark to sit back at the table and keep coloring.

MY MOTHER WAS NOT SO EASILY DISSUADED. She wanted to know everything about Mark, where he'd grown up, what he did, if he liked it, the last president he'd voted for—by the time dinner was ready, the only thing she didn't know was his astrological sign.

"Really, Mom," I said, trying to cut her off.

"I just need to know what his thoughts are on global warming—"

"Mother!"

"We live in the desert, honey—it's not going to get better here unless the world does—"

Mark chuckled and gave me an amused look. "It's okay. I'm a lawyer, remember? I'm good at asking—and answering—questions."

"The only questions I want answered now is, 'Does this taste good', with a side of 'How was school today?'" I walked over to the table, pot in hand.

"School was fine," Rabbit said.

"Just fine?"

"Molly tried to beat me up again."

"A girl?" Mark asked.

Rabbit hunched over a little, his body expressing his dismay. "She's really mean. And twice as big as I am."

"She was held back," I explained and squeezed Rabbit's hand. "I'll talk to the teacher tomorrow."

"That doesn't do anything," Rabbit protested.

"I used to get beat up at school a lot," Mark volunteered.

Rabbit looked up at him, this man who made our dining room look small. "Really?"

"Yeah."

"How'd you stop it?" Rabbit asked.

"Well, eventually I grew too big. But I spent all of middle school hiding in the library for lunch—until I made enough friends to protect me. When you have more friends than the bullies do, you're usually all right."

Rabbit considered this. "I hang out with Michael and Chapman, we try to protect each other."

"You're on the way then. I bet you're not the only kids Molly's mean to. Find the other ones and help them out."

Rabbit nodded, shoving a forkful of spaghetti into his mouth. "This is good, Mom."

I looked around the table at my motley crew. "Yeah, it is."

ONCE DINNER WAS OVER, I had time to trim the flowers he'd brought. My mother made a show of going back to the TV room to give us 'privacy' and Rabbit wanted to play Minecraft online with this buddies upstairs.

"You shouldn't have," I said, clipping the second to last rose.

"Hey, if they've been watching you, they know we're dating. And me being here gives my driver an excuse to stay in the parking lot."

"Your driver?"

"A friend of mine."

"Watching out."

"Precisely."

I felt bad for him, whoever he was, trapped outside in the cold in a car. "Should we take him some spaghetti?"

"He's good, I promise."

I settled the roses into a vase. "Did I overhear you telling my son to form a gang?"

He laughed. "Not in so many words, no."

"Just checking," I said, smiling over the roses at him. There was still the unopened bottle of wine. "Should we?" I asked.

He gave me a wicked smile. "I'm not going anywhere."

"Then open this while I get Rabbit into the bath." I handed him the bottle and a corkscrew and walked upstairs.

I HERDED Rabbit back and forth between his bedroom and the bathroom, until he was finally tucked in bed.

"Mom," he whispered, as I walked for the door.

"What?" I'd already read him a short book—if he asked for a longer one I'd have to put my foot down.

"What about my vitamins?"

I stood there with my hand on the light switch. The temptation to let him skip a day was huge—I didn't want to run down and then back up, that might invite questions. But I knew how bad my wolf was after a day. One day off, and I bet his wolf would have him egging Molly on, hoping for a fight.

"Sure thing, baby, I'll be right back."

I went downstairs and found my mother and Mark in deep conversation, waved to show I wasn't done yet, grabbed the silver, and raced back upstairs to give Rabbit his eyedropper full. He still didn't like them, but he liked being babied by me, he was still my little boy. I smooched his head, and turned his light off, and listened at the door until I was sure he'd stayed in bed.

When I came back down the stairs my mother made a show of being tired, out-stretched arms, oversized yawns and all, taking herself off to her room to sleep, as I settled down in a chair.

"Could she be any more obvious?"

"I like her. I like him." He reached for the bottle and poured me a glass. I eyed the bottle to see how far ahead of me he was, if my mother had driven him to drink. "Your mother told me where these were," he said, pushing one over. "And now that we both have glasses, I want to propose a toast."

"Oh?"

"Cento di questi giorni," he said.

"What's that?" I liked the sound of it.

"To a hundred days like this."

I looked over at Mark, appearing content inside my kitchen. "Indeed." I clinked my glass to his, and sipped.

CHAPTER NINETEEN
JACK

The night air didn't phase me. I lay down on the strip mall's roof, staring up at the clear Vegas sky, lit by the belly of the moon. Murphy was still behind me, pacing, smoking, pacing again—I'd always know where he was as long as I could smell him and his cigar.

Had there been a cigar scent at Bella's? No. But I was okay with creating some collateral terror as I worked my way back to killing the right Pack boss. To my mind, all of them had been involved.

I watched the stars turn until my flesh was almost as cold as the night itself, when I heard Murphy prepare to leave, saying as much to a subordinate. Then I leapt up, and raced for the far end of the roof where I'd parked my car. I turned my engine over as he turned his, masking my sound with his own, and as his motorcycle pulled out from the thinned herd of chrome, I followed.

I wanted to see which way he was going first—I knew crime paid well enough, but I was curious if Murphy would let that show— nothing like buying too nice a house to interest the IRS. Instead of driving into Vegas, he drove out, toward the surrounding desert. Maybe he wanted to commune with his conscience under the moonlight. I followed at a distance without headlights, but when he pulled over, I turned them on and drove up, slowing down, blocking his bike in with my car.

I stopped, opened my car door to stand halfway out, and pretended to be companionable. "Did you break down?"

My arrival startled him. Whatever he'd been doing—something involving the front of his shirt—he stopped and looked guilty. "I'm fine—go away."

"Afraid I can't." I propelled myself over the hood of my car to land feet first on the other side. "Does the name Bella ring any bells?"

"Shit—" He tossed a leg over his motorcycle—I ran up and kicked his back tire, hard enough to bend his rim. He didn't let it fall though, he fought my momentum, holding it upright. His hands went to bags as I leaned in to punch him.

The man had a jaw like a piece of granite. And my punch should've taken him down—but all it did was knock him off his bike. He stumbled backwards but didn't fall, even as his motorcycle tipped over. "Who the fuck are you?" he said, holding his jaw.

"A concerned friend." I kicked his motorcycle out of the way, sending it ten feet out into the street. "What happened to her? What'd she want with you?"

He looked from his bike to me. "How the fuck—who are you?"

"What happened to her?" I repeated in a low growl, bringing the full force of my whammy to bear.

He blinked, momentarily mesmerized. "We had her for months. She never mentioned a boyfriend."

"Had?" I asked archly, still using my powers. His answer would determine how many of his bones I broke before killing him.

Then he shook himself. I didn't think he should've been able to, but he did. No matter, there were other ways of getting information.

I jumped him.

Neither of us were pretty fighters, none of the graceful shit you see on TV. We were bred for the pits, and acted like it. I was taller than he was and had better reach, but he was fucking sturdy in a way

I'd never seen. Blows that would've incapacitated a normal man did nothing to him, while he rained heavy fists on me any time he got close. I just needed to get him down into a headlock—I saw an opening and took it, but he punched back, just in time. I dodged it, but a rock slid out from under my boot, making me drop my guard. His next punch landed hard, and I felt ribs snap.

I clutched a hand to my chest. As a vampire, I'd never had anyone hurt me before. *What the fuck are you?* I wanted to ask him—then I realized if I kept staying alive, he'd ask the same of me. He turned and ran –

"Oh no you don't—" I said and leapt for him—as he dove for his bags and brought a sawed off shotgun up. I had time for the weapon to register, right before he shot me. Catching a chest full of lead, I fell.

I...was injured. Not dying, but...hurt. It was an entirely new sensation for me. I rose up onto my elbows and looked down at myself. Blood, precious blood—mostly other people's—leaking out, scattershot on my chest, literally. I didn't know what to do—should I pretend to be mortally wounded? Would he know what I was if I didn't? Would he come and try to finish the job?

How come I hadn't finished him?

Rage boiled in me then, even as blood sieved out. I wanted him to die—and I needed to drink him, to make up for what I'd lost. I stood up and lurched forward. He tried to shoot me again, but he'd used his last shot. Must've missed reloading day at Biker Boy Scouts. He was breathing hard, like I was—I'd hurt him more than he'd let on, one eye swelling shut, blood dripping from where I'd broken his nose, his free hand wrapped around to guard his liver. A wind struck up, wafted the scent of his fear to me, and I laughed. Vampirism offered few true joys, but getting to occasionally be exceptionally creepy and laugh like a maniac was one of them.

I smiled at him wickedly. "Tell me what happened to Bella, or I'll pull you apart and suck the marrow from your bones."

His eyes widened, and he stumbled up. I'd been in fights like this before. He'd fight erratically now, too panicked to defend. All of them ended in only one delicious way.

But instead of coming for me—he turned tail and ran. Not toward his bike or my car, but out into the desert. I lunged after him —and felt things grind inside, bone on bone—and my hunger that'd been kept in abeyance by Paco's blood and sex exploded, now that I was several pints low. I could use that energy to chase after him— but I couldn't guarantee what condition I'd be in when I caught up. If it took over—the hunger was savage, and I wanted answers, not to just cover myself in blood and make his corpse look like it'd been dropped from 500 feet up.

Goddammit!

I stumbled back to my car, popped the trunk, grabbed a trash bag, and threw it over the driver's seat like someone who'd had to do this more than once before, and got in.

CHAPTER TWENTY
ANGELA

"I'm glad you have a driver," I told Mark. We'd almost reached the bottle of wine's end. Neither one of us had brought up the elephant in the room—what'd happened this morning, and what Mark was presumably going to do about it. Maybe he'd already set things in motion. I sent my finger swirling along the rim of my wine glass, wondering if I wanted to ask.

He finished off his glass and set it back down. "Did you do what I told you to do?"

I looked up at him and then down again, flushing, not just from the wine. I'd thought about it, twice, when the panic had started to rise—picturing myself in his office again, my thighs pressed against the sharp edge of his desk as he took my ass, something we hadn't yet done, imagining feeling myself filled by him someplace new. "Yes," I answered, a truthful whisper.

"Did it help?"

I nodded faintly.

"Good."

I'd had enough wine to feel a little spinny, but not so much as to make bad decisions, and I knew that as I looked over at him. "Would you like to spend the night?"

A knowing smile spread across his face. "I would."

At that, I put one finger to my lips for quiet, and stood and took his hand.

HALFWAY UP THE STAIRS, his hands were on my ass. I slapped them away, then finished pulling him to my room, past Rabbit's and the bathroom's door. My bedroom was not set up for company, I had dresses all over a decorating screen, a vanity full of potions, and my queen didn't look big enough for the both of us. He walked in and looked around, naturally gravitating toward the bed.

"I feel like I'm in high school."

"Me too." I felt like I'd just snuck a boy in. "I've never brought anyone home before. So, uh, welcome to me." I spun around, indicating my four walls.

He made a show of pacing the room, stopping in front of a framed 12 x 12 painting of a curled and sleeping rabbit, so perfect that only brush strokes proved it wasn't a photo. "That's lovely—is it your work?"

"Jack made it for me," I said. "A long time ago."

"Ahh." He surveyed everything else in silence, stopping only to close the blinds on my windows. I knew what he meant by it—he didn't want anyone to see us fuck—but I still didn't know what I was hoping for. I got the sex. I'd always gotten the sex. But him, here, really knowing me? Except for the werewolf part....

The wine made me do it. "Mark—why me?"

He turned back from his inspection of my belongings, looking over a shelf of clay animals that Rabbit had crafted and I'd kept. "What?"

"I mean—I'm a hassle."

He smiled. "A sexy hassle."

"This is Vegas. It's pretty easy to find hassle-free sex here."

His head tilted as he considered me. "I want to help you."

"I know you do. But before all that, and before this morning. I know why I want to be with you—you're smart and handsome, you make me laugh, and we are epic in bed. But—why would someone like you want to be with me?"

He sat down on my bed in front of me. "I've been here for a while, ever since my uncle told me to come out here and go to law school." He put his hands behind him, leaning back into my unmade bed. "I spent a long time doing things I shouldn't have. Things I thought would make me happy. I had a really fierce coke habit. Not because I even really liked it, but because of who I was and who I hung with, it was expected of me. After I flunked out of school though—I don't know, I realized I wasn't happy. I stopped the coke, switched schools and started studying. It took me awhile longer to get over my show-girl habit, but I kicked them too." His lips curved into a gentle smile. "All day long I talk to people who have something to prove, guys who want to chest bump me, and women who live plastic lives. And you? You're like this whirlwind of reality. You get what's important in life. I love that your kid matters to you, more than anything—more than me. That you care about, and take care of, your mom. I don't want to take you away from all this—I just want to add to it."

My heart swelled to bursting. And he pushed himself forward, I thought to stand, but instead he went down on his knees.

"Come here," he said, and I did, stepping forward.

He knelt, his hands starting at my calves, running down them to unlace my sandals, helping me to kick them off, one by one, and then he began to touch me. His hands trailed slowly, like he was a sculptor, molding me, stroking my calves one by one, then tracing the backs of my knees, before coming around to push up my thighs, his thumbs coming dangerously close, before he pushed back to palm the curve of my ass and reach up, up, up to finger the waistband of my underwear and tug.

He pulled the cotton down with just as much care as he'd stroked up, deliberately, like he was unwrapping a present the old fashioned way, saving the wrapping paper. I wanted to help him, to shuck it off and skip to what I hoped was coming—but I loved how he was taking his time. I shifted from foot to foot, helping him free me from the thin cotton chain, then he looked up.

"Pull your skirt up for me, Angie."

I whispered, "Okay," and held my skirt up like a peasant girl stepping over a puddle, as he leaned forward to kiss the insides of my thighs.

I gasped lightly—I'd known this was coming, and yet—I spread my legs to make more room, to show him more of me. He took one of my thighs in both of his hands and started kissing, nuzzling me up from my knee. I could feel the roughness of his beard's shadow chasing the heat of his breath from each kiss as his hands crawled up, moving now to push my thighs apart. I arched toward him, and he murmured his assent into my thigh, creeping ever higher until he was looking up at me, his amber eyes dark, and my pussy aching. One hand reached up to press up my stomach and stretch me up, the other held a thigh. Pinned between his hands, his mouth came up and kissed.

Mark slid the flat of his tongue across my clit, forward and back, rolling it out from under its hood. If he could just keep doing that, stay there like some delicious machine made for my pleasure—I went weak in the knees and moaned softly.

He rose up and came closer, to kiss more of me, to move his tongue more roughly as his lips sucked and pulled me open. His chin ground up and in and I was not ladylike in the way I pressed down to give him more. I couldn't help but watch him—my strong and dangerous giant, tamed enough to kneel to take me. No, not tamed, but confident. To know that he knew what I wanted, and how best to give it to me. I shuddered with a sudden release of power, feeling safe, feeling—possessed—and—I dropped my skirt and wound both my hands into his hair and started to ride. He grabbed hold of my ass, the strength of his grip betraying his urgency.

I started to use his mouth like I might a toy, thinking only of myself. I closed my eyes and pulled him harder onto me, grinding my clit against his tongue, listening to him purr as my wetness flowed down around his chin, his stubble pressing perfectly against me. His hand on my thigh slid in and he set his thumb inside my pussy, giving me both more and less leverage as I rocked.

I was using him shamelessly—and he liked it. Every throb, every rock, every lick that pushed me closer to the cliff—his mouth and hands worked in synchrony, me and my body just holding on. He knew exactly what he was doing and was going to keep on doing it until—I rose up on my toes again, this time my ass clenched and wouldn't stop tensing and everything in me narrowed to one shining spot that he claimed with his tongue and —my hands clenched in his hair. "Mark," I hissed low, bucking my clit against his tongue. "Mark—" I said, even louder, then bit my lips to stay quiet, as my orgasm made me reel. I shuddered over him, hips twitching, me trying to stifle small sounds as my body tensed and released over and over again. When the last of it was wrung out of me, he leaned back looking smug, and I sagged, slumping down as he caught me, my skirt billowing innocently out.

He held me against his chest, in his lap, me breathless. His face was half-wet, and I knew that sensitive parts of me would have beard-burn tomorrow. I leaned up to kiss him, and he kissed me back, true and deep, before I fell back again in exhaustion, and he moved to lean us both against my bed.

"I like it when you taste like me," I murmured into his chest, dreamily.

"Since I like tasting you, that works out nicely."

The light from the streetlight outside peeked in through my blinds and made stripes on his face. "I'm not sure what I did to deserve you."

He brushed my hair back and kissed my forehead. "You let the right stranger buy you a drink?"

"I didn't even want to go out that night. But my mom told me I shouldn't miss Jenny's party—"

I heard his chest rumble as he chuckled, and slowly I inhabited my body again. I was curled up against him—it was easy for me to wriggle my hand down between us just right—and he made a pleased sound as my hand grazed the inseam of his slacks.

"As much as I want to desecrate your bedroom, in all sorts of ways—" he pushed me forward. "I can't stay here tonight."

I pursed my lips and gave him a challenging glare. "Is that how long you think it'd take me?"

His resolve melted, as I felt him get harder. I crawled out of his lap without moving my hand, as if breaking my connection might give him permission to go. Then I arranged myself in front of him, kneeling down, like a cross between a supplicant and a cat, and with skillful fingers, undid his belt, the latch of his slacks, and zipped everything down.

His cock came out. I'd seen it at least fifty times now, and yet every time I saw it still felt new. I loved everything about it: the way it fit in me like a key to a lock, the solid weight of it when he rammed it between my thighs, how its skin was hot and soft, the way I could touch it and know what he was thinking. I leaned forward on elbows and breathed over it without touching, promising him more.

For his part, he was still—as still as I had been earlier, when he'd been touching me—the same disbelief I'd felt, mirrored in his eyes. We were both bad at this, at the softer things in life, at trusting. But we both wanted to. I knew I did—and I knew he did, as I kissed the smooth underbelly of his cock and he sighed and closed his eyes.

I covered it in a thousand tender kisses, feeling it bob and sway, like a snake looking for purchase up a cliff. I had all the time in the world to give it attention, and listening to Mark gasp and groan was music to my ears. And just when I thought he wouldn't take anymore, when my delicacy would drive him literally wild, I brought my lips down to kiss his head.

I swirled my tongue in ever widening circles, lowering my mouth onto him, taking his head in, as he whispered, "Oh Angela," harshly. I could see his hands winding in my sheets, as he held onto either side of my bed like a prisoner, trying to stop himself from grabbing my hair and forcing me down.

I slid down him as far as I could bear, in one long continuous suck, feeling his cock bend at the back of my throat, and then pulled off of him, just as slow, relishing the taste of precum.

"Angela," he moaned again, staring frankly at me now. I knew what he wanted, what his eyes asked, and pulled off of his cock entirely.

"Remember, my room's not soundproof," I warned with a wicked grin, and kept on.

I took him in long, elaborate sucks, letting him in a little further each time, ignoring the way I was covering him in spit, feeling his ass twitch as he tried to control the destiny of his own cock, unable to stop himself from thrusting. Then I reached back and pulled my skirt up again, so he could see the heart shaped curve of my ass as I bowed low, and he groaned like he'd been defeated. I chuckled, lifted off of him, and started sucking on his balls.

"Oh God, Angie—" he reached for his cock with one hand and started stroking fast.

"Hmm?" I purred, without stopping, taking one of his balls into my mouth completely, rubbing my tongue against its soft-rough side.

His hips betrayed him again, I heard his breathing speed up— and there was no way I was going to let him finish himself without me. I pushed his hand away and took his cock over with my mouth, bobbing and sucking, pressing my tongue up against his shaft from the very bottom to the top. His hands wound in my hair, pulling me down, and my wolf loved this—she loved being made to gag. I groaned in pleasure as he warned, "Angie—I'm going to," and I felt him stiffen one last time, before gasping, as hot salty silver jetted into my mouth. I took it and kept sucking him, like I wanted more, sucking him through it. When he stopped thrusting and went soft then and only then did I pull back.

He looked like I'd felt thirty minutes ago, collapsed against the side of my bed. I rearranged my skirt and gave him a smug grin. "So you can go home now, if you want to."

He blinked and grinned back. "You're evil, you know that?"

"No, I'm good. Very, very good." I traced a finger down his chest. "And now that you're here, I don't want you to go away."

"I don't want to go either. But we have to pace ourselves. Make things seem normal." He set himself back inside his pants, locking himself back up with his zipper, then reached a hand out to me, which I took. "And then once things really are normal—nothing will ever keep me away."

"Promise?"

"I swear." He brought his other hand up to my cheek and traced it. "But for now, missy," he said while standing, pulling me up after him, "you need to get to bed. But don't take any clothes off right now —if you do I'll never find the strength to leave."

I crossed my arms belligerently. "I'll take pity on you, this time. Only once though."

"Thanks," he said, coming in for a kiss.

We stumbled down the stairs, kissing and groping, unable to let tonight finish, until his coat was on and he was at my door, kissing me against it, one hand on the knob, unable to leave me.

"I want you again, Angela," he said, his breath hot on my neck.

"I want you too," I whispered back, having visions of him taking me here in my kitchen, on all fours on the tile. Then there was a sound above us, and we both froze, the spell momentarily broken. I used the opportunity to dart away—I couldn't do anything wild like that where Rabbit would find out. And if he heard us and woke up all the way now—the thought of that was like cold water down my spine.

Mark was not similarly tortured, and took a step near, closing the space between us until I put a hand out to stop him. "You have to go."

"I do," he reluctantly agreed.

"Promise me one more thing first?"

"Anything."

"If you touch yourself again tonight, you have to think of me."

A sly smile crossed his face. "I would have, anyways."

I grinned back at him, helplessly, not trusting myself to kiss him again. "Go on then. Get."

He leaned in and kissed me one more time, before finally leaving.

CHAPTER TWENTY-ONE
JACK

There was only one place in Vegas I could go to in this condition, one person that would understand, who wouldn't ask questions, mostly. Francesca's.

Francesca's place occupied a small office park, and all the offices were technically there for business, just not the kind that required secretaries or HR. Or maybe they did, I really wasn't up to date on Las Vegas tax codes where sex dungeons were concerned. I parked my car in the back, walked past a row of rentals, the occasional Tesla, and one very out of place mini-van, before knocking on a completely nondescript door.

I knew someone was looking at me through the one-way glass on the other side, then I heard a key move a lock, and Vincent's face loomed, the bouncer for tonight.

"You look like shit."

"Thank you for stating the obvious, Vincent. Is the lady in?"

"Of course. She's busy though."

The hunger wound its way up through my gut and into my chest. It would be so easy to push the door open and bleed him. "Can you get me a room?"

"As a favored freak, yes."

He undid another lock which let the door further open—if you were going to clean up before a raid, you needed all the excuses to slowly lawfully cooperate you could find—and I slid in.

Francesca's entry way was done in tastefully minimalist décor, like an upscale spa, and there was a well-dressed secretary frowning at me from the far side of a polished desk. "Jack," she tsked.

"Janice," I acknowledged her with a tight smile, and tried to ignore the way my hunger coiled, waiting.

"This way," Vincent said, and led me down the hall.

The building still retained its general office-like nature, but Franny had made a ton of upgrades, from replacing the shitty drop down ceiling with stamped tin and soundproofing all the doors. Every window we passed was tinted, except for the ones of people paying extra for the thrill of being seen.

Despite Franny's best efforts, I could still smell what went on here, the dual scents of want and need. This place'd been going for so long, they'd probably never air out.

Vincent opened a door revealing a cramped room full of metal shelves with bottles on them, brooms and mops. "You can wait in here."

"Is this a closet?"

"You'd be surprised how many affairs start in office closets. Sometimes people like to reminisce."

I stared at him. His face was so implacable, I could never tell when he was joking. Vincent was the living embodiment of the words 'seen it all'.

"Sure." I wasn't in any position to argue. I went in and sat down, all the better to keep my remaining blood inside me. At least this room was windowless. "Tell Fran to hurry, will you?"

"Will do," he said, then both closed and locked the door, which I was grateful for. I lay down and tried to meditate my hunger away.

CHAPTER TWENTY-ONE

THIS WAS AN ONLY RECENTLY ACQUIRED skill. I knew certain vampires managed to perform something like suspended animation, to find freedom from the urge to feed by drastically slowing down. I hadn't figured out all the kinks yet, but I wanted to.

I'd never been addicted to anything in real life—the life I'd had before my vampirism. But I'd known enough addicts, closely, to know that that's what this was like. This whole-body longing, every cell calling, down to the fiber of my theoretically lost soul. Everything in me wanted to feed, and not just feed, but glory in the blood. Make a show of taking it, run someone down, them knowing they were going to die just as I knew I was going to kill them. To wait until the last possible moment when they were trembling helplessly in my arms and bite. To taste their salt-bitter-sour, like sucking on pennies, the heat of their blood on my tongue. To feel the stillness emanate from them as they died, as the life they'd possessed poured into me. Did Paco know how close he'd been to dying—I'd bitten him at least a hundred times—when if for a second I let the hunger rule me it would take him? I thought maybe he did. Maybe it was why he loved me. I was the personification of his secret wish to die, more dangerous than any gun.

I visualized my hunger as an amorphous beast, an animal I could not fully comprehend, like something swimming in the deep ocean, and tried to let it wash over me. Yes, it was everywhere, yes it was all the time, but we were separate, it and I. I could acknowledge it and move on. I could stay still, battered by its waves, yet remain afloat.

I was concentrating so hard on this that I didn't know how much time had passed when I next woke.

"Jack?" said a melodious voice.

I blinked awake—the hunger had abated, somewhat—and my nice leather jacket was in tatters around my arm, cut up to the elbow, where Franny had inserted an IV. Red cabled down from a bag of blood like licorice.

"You're on your second," she informed me.

141

And after that, I noticed the blindfolded woman at my hips, kneeling politely, stroking my cock.

"Franny," I complained, swatting the woman's hand aside.

"Hey Jack," the woman said, companionably.

"Sarah? Sarah." I recognized the curve of her smile and the straightness of her hair. "Goddammit."

"Don't be angry. She's blindfolded. And if anyone knows the value of a good blindfold, it's me."

I gave Franny a look that was supposed to convey, *How many more people need to know my secret?* While Franny telegraphed back, *Look, you're the one who showed up here half-dead,* with an arch of a well-plucked eyebrow.

I rocked back and pulled up my pants, as Francesca stood and gave the IV bag a squeeze, pulsing more blood into my arm. Tonight she was wearing completely skin-tight latex, from her ankles to neck —I had no idea how she got into or out of the thing, I supposed she had helpers for that, and was wearing a fabulous wig of curly blonde hair which poofed out evenly on all sides. She'd chosen C-cups for the evening, but I'd seen her before in falsies all the way out to GG's, with complicated non-BDSM harnesses behind her back.

Once upon a time, Francesca had been Frank, which was when we'd met, becoming fast friends after I'd given him a late-night tattoo. Perhaps he'd sensed the deviancy from the norm in me, or I in him, but he'd trusted me enough to tell me when his gender and his occupation changed: from a moderately good EMS tech to an amazingly good drag queen and master of a series of increasingly nicer dungeons, culminating in this one here. Somewhere along the way I'd come clean myself—I think right after Franny explained medical play. Some people were into bloody kinks. It wasn't a guaranteed thing—but if she ever got any, she froze it special in a locked freezer and texted me. Blood divorced from consequences and guilt? Sign me the hell up.

Fran took the bag off the pole and rolled it like a tube of toothpaste, pushing the last of the contents inside me. I felt much, much better now—looking down, I could see the holes on my shirt where the lead'd gone in, but only smooth skin lay behind. Eventually I'd cough up the buckshot or shit them out—being a vampire was odd. And where my ribs had been rubbing, they were solid now, I gave them a poke. Fran chased the last bit of blood into me, then pulled out the IV, wheeling the whole contraption into the back, hiding it behind a shelf.

"You can get up now, Sarah."

"Thank you, Mistress," she said, rising as smooth as any geisha. She didn't move like I'd have moved, stretching out kinks. The only thing she had to betray she'd ever been uncomfortably sitting for so long were red spots on her knees, clearly visible beneath her short-short skirt.

"You may take off your blindfold and leave."

"Thank you, Mistress."

Sarah did as she was told. She looked at me, and gave me a satis-fied smile—Sarah was a service sub, through and through. The men of Vegas's tourism had little use for her, as most of them longed to be dominated themselves, but when she performed for the right dom, she was spectacular.

"Till next time, Jack," she said, lunging in for a kiss, before racing for the door.

She was also a little bit of a brat.

Francesca turned back to me, and gave me a look. "You don't call, you don't write—and then you show up, looking like that?"

"I'm sorry, Fran. I've been busy and...." Telling her everything would feel good. I wanted to understand what the hell had happened—why that strange biker hadn't died. But her eyes squinted at me and her red lips curled into an appeasing grin. "What?" I asked, a little nervously.

"You know how you're always saying you owe me?"

I suddenly wondered if I'd made the right choice, not chasing Murphy into the desert. "Yeah?"

"Time to pay up. And then I'll hear all about whatever the hell happened to you later tonight. I'm interested, darling, I am, but you coming here is something of a godsend."

And knowing what went on inside these walls.... "How so?"

"I've got a couple. They're new to me—"but they both claim to want a cuckold."

"Ugh, Franny—"

"No. It's perfect. You're scary enough that she won't say yes unless she's really into it. And behind one way glass, he can beat off confidently, knowing that a mom of three isn't going to leave him for you. You being who you are, of course." She waved a hand to indicate my intricate tattoos.

It was ironic, considering the woman I'd lusted after longest without success was also a mother. But what would Angela think of me, if she knew what I was?

"Plus you're all I've got. They rolled in late, no appointments. Rude, but with a lot of cash. So," she said, grabbing my arm and propelling me down the hall. "Take a shower and then get in there, slugger."

FRANCESCA HAD THOUGHT OF EVERYTHING—THE showers were just as nice as the rest of the rooms here, except for the rooms that were disgusting on purpose of course. I thought they might be for employees, then realized it was possible people wanted to enact assorted shower-scenes like they'd watched in porn. I opened a fresh bar of soap and scrubbed up.

I'd read somewhere once that 'Mood's a thing for cattle,' meaning that one ought to always be in control of one's self. Self-aware adults don't always get the luxury of feeling out of sorts—or headachy, as the case may be. And tonight, neither did I. I turned the water off, and reached for a towel.

Franny had put out a blood-free outfit for me to wear, much like the one I'd lost—jeans, T-shirt, white this time, and another black leather jacket. The shirt and jeans didn't really fit, too small and too big in turns, but the jacket—I ran a hand over the smooth leather after I put it on.

"Exceptional. As always," Fran said, coming into the room she'd led me to.

"This is what I'm wearing in their fantasy?" I found that hard to believe.

"Don't worry, it doesn't have to stay on long."

A bed occupied the center of the room, neatly made with nice sheets, a nightstand on each side, and a leather chair sat in the corner.

"Is that where he's going to be?"

"No. I've arranged the cameras for him." She pointed at the ceiling, where small red lights shone.

"Is he up there already?"

"Ready and waiting."

I strode over to the chair, sat down, slung a leg over an arm, and looked up at the nearest camera. "Thanks for letting me fuck your wife," I said loudly.

"Jack!" Franny protested.

I gave her a bemused look. "That's what he wants, isn't it?"

"You are incorrigible." She put her hands on her hips, surveyed the room, and then nodded to herself, satisfied. I was glad one of us was. I watched her walk out.

Living in Vegas I was well aware of all the different ways that sex could be transactional, from the brothels far outside of town, the card-clickers on the corners creating litter, to the vast abyss of the internet. Anything from a blow-job to an orgy could be bought here, including, apparently, me.

I was slouching into the chair, trying to look like I did this sort of thing all the time, when she walked in.

She was as tall as I was, thin and angular like a ballerina, her chest almost flat. Her hair was in a flapper-ish dark brown bob—all the better to be out of children's sticky hands. She had on khaki trousers and, I swear to God, a mint green sweater set, pearl buttons clasped all the way up. There was a ring on her finger, and her thin lips were pulled into a worried line. She stood just inside the doorway, and I could feel her judging me.

Time to cut to the chase. "Is this really your idea of a good time?" It was easy for me to act like I didn't care, because I honestly didn't— after the bleeding I'd taken Franny had tanked me half-a-pint up.

Her lips quirked and her eyes narrowed. "Is it yours?"

I tilted my head and let my eyes roam her body. Everything about her said *control-control-control*. Her hair was precise, her clothing the kind that old money wore, her children likely headed to Ivy Leagues. To break a woman like that—let it never be said that I shirked a challenge. "It could be." I unslung my leg, but kept myself relaxed. "So what've you and he negotiated? What's he want to see down here?"

"Me. Being with some other man." Her jaw clenched a little, and she glanced at the floor, before remembering her pride and glaring back up.

"That's it?"

She swallowed and nodded.

"There's a lot of some other men in the world. Which one would you like?" I hadn't moved a muscle, nor was I going to, until I'd sussed her out.

"I—I don't know."

I made a thoughtful noise, then played for the camera. "Then let's talk about that. Because I do like the idea of him up there, watching helplessly, as I ravage his beautiful wife—the one that no one would ever imagine cheating on him. But if she were ever going too...." I let my voice drift and kept watching her intently. "Should I be a man who picked you up someplace plain? Like the grocery store? You and I, standing in different isles with a pile of apples between us, and we both look up. Something electric happens then, a charge carried by our eyes, something physical or chemical. You know that I want you, and worse yet, that you want me. You try to ignore it, but you can't. You look away, but you still see me in your mind. When you look up, I'm gone, but that night you touch yourself, imagining me—knowing, hoping, that somewhere out there I'm stroking myself to my memory of you."

I had more than enough blood on board to whammy her, but apart from the fact I wouldn't have—I didn't have to. I could tell she was falling under the spell of the rhythm of my words, see her breathing change to match the pacing of my story.

"Or do we meet at a cocktail party? Maybe one your husband's also at? It's very fancy, a celebration, everyone's in tuxes or satin. I'm not invited of course—I'm working, anonymously. But I brush past you, bringing out more champagne, and for a moment I touch your hip, just to warn you that I'm there. You gasp, surprised, and whirl, but I'm already serving other guests—except that I look back at you. The place I touched you somehow burns—the same way my gaze rolling over you makes you feel all over. You're conscious of my place in the room and everyone else in it, and know that your husband's not there, he's off talking some sort of drab business with a friend. And so you crook your finger at me, and like a good servant I follow."

She was breathing harder now, imagining herself. I felt her flush more than saw it, read the patterns of heat of her rising blood.

"We go into the first empty room we find. It's a child's room...."

She gasps like I hoped she would. "I would never do that!"

"How can you be so sure?" I say, with utter confidence and a wicked smile. "Is there nothing you've ever wanted in your life so badly that you had to have it now?"

She doesn't answer me, she just rocks back and forth a little—but the heat of her blood doesn't fade.

"You push me to the ground," I go on. "I know what you want and I'm willing to give it, and you stand over me with your shiny short skirt and kneel down, reaching between your legs to set me into you as I take your shoulders with both hands and thrust up. The shadows of everything lit by only a night light are strangely beautiful across your body and my face. You ride me wildly, ferociously, knowing that somewhere out there your husband is milling, possibly even now searching for you, asking if anyone knows where you went. You know you have only moments to keep feeling this alive—and you're smart enough to not even kiss me, because that would mess your make-up up. You just want now, and this, and this, and this."

Her mouth opened a little as her jaw dropped.

"Or perhaps I could be some other-other man? Did you go with him on a business trip? And then walk down the wrong alley? Have I spotted you, like some kind of prey? What if I grab you there and make you feel me? Have I kidnapped you and now all my mercy depends on how well you suck my cock?"

At this, her breath caught. I still hadn't moved, I was still waiting for her—and then trembling hands went to the top of her sweater. That was my signal. I stood up and came over to her and picked her up, throwing her onto the bed, following her instantly. Our clothed bodies pressed together as my mouth met hers and I kissed her hard. She stiffened in surprise—but then began to kiss me back. Hands that were still trembling began to touch me, searching up under my shirt and on top of the denim of my jeans. I reared up to throw my jacket off, and then set to work on the tiny pearl buttons, snapping the threads of as many as I managed to open, and then helped her shuck the camisole underneath off.

Her bra was a lacy thing, no wires, no cups—I pushed it up and took her small breasts into my mouth, one by one, almost whole, like I was eating them. She moaned at this, running her hands through my hair—and then sending them down my back to claw my t-shirt up. I rose again to pull it off, and she gasped again at seeing me.

Sometimes I forgot that my skin's somewhat of a spectacle.

I watched her reach out a tentative hand to touch the skull that lay on my chest, down my stomach, and lower. Somehow, I doubted that her husband looked like me, and who knew the last time she'd touched another man. I waited and when her hand was already low, I took it lower, planting it on the outside of my jeans against my cock.

Did he, whoever he was, ever want her like this? He did in a theoretical sense, seeing as he was watching. But was that his whole thing? Did he close his eyes when he fucked her, imagining watching someone else doing the deed, him peeking through the slats of a closet door?

I looked down at her, half-naked, sheets of the bed already wrinkling. I knew what I wanted her to do with her hand next, but first I reached down and touched her ring-finger with its oversized diamond.

"On, or off?"

She swallowed, as if this one thing made it all real.

"Off," she said, taking it off, setting it safely in a pocket. Then I took her hand back and slid it into my pants and her fingers obligingly wrapped around my cock.

I wanted her to feel me before she saw me. I started back in on her chest, my hands working the buckle for her thin tan belt, freeing it, and then unlatching her trousers so I could also reach inside. Hands were good—hands were safe—and this might be as far as we got before he called it off—I wanted to give him a good long ride, but with plenty of exits, if either of them didn't feel right. I was just a bit player, but they had to manage to look at each other in the morning.

I slowly pushed my hand in through untamed fur—a confident 70's bush—and let my fingers curl, finding soft folds of skin. Her breath caught in surprise—and then mine did, as she started to tentatively stroke me. She looked up at this, realizing she also had power—that this erection, my erection, was here for her to use. And at that, I swirled my hand gently, rubbing her clit softly once, twice, before pushing a finger in.

Her pussy was as wet as I knew it'd be, once I'd parted her folds. I used that wetness, stroking up, to lubricate her clit with my fingers, listening to her moan. I leaned down, nuzzling her breasts again, stroking her as she stroked me, thrusting gently into her hand. I couldn't help myself. I wanted more.

She turned the tables and brought her hand up to take my precum and swirl it over the head of me, making me moan into her. And then she pulled her hand out and set it on my belt buckle.

"Yeah?" I asked her quietly.

"Yes," she whispered back.

I rose up over her to my full height and leaned back to open the drawer of the nightstand, finding an assortment of condoms, lube, and toys. I pulled out three condoms and brought them back.

She'd wriggled out of the top of her slacks and underwear like a teenager in the back of a car—I got off the bed, and helped her finish the job, tugging both off of her, then divested my own with slightly more dignity. She crawled up the bed while watching me with eagle eyes, and I could see the patterns of her blood inside her, almost like a dark arrow pointing down to her hips. I took one of the condoms, opened it up, pulled it on—in full view of several cameras—and then mounted the bed.

Her knees came up, and I set my hands on them, waiting for permission to push them wide and enter her, to the hilt, my cock already throbbing with need.

Her heart fluttered and her eyes shone. "Can—can you be very gentle?" she asked me.

I sat back a little. "Of course."

At my agreement, she nodded, and opened her legs slowly, revealing everything inside. I moved over her body with my own, my arms on either side of her chest, letting my cock swing between us, rubbing it against her pussy without going in.

"You can tell me anything. Faster, slower, harder, softer, all right?" I told her, and she nodded. With that, I pulled back my hips enough to guide my head into her soft heat.

"Oh," she whispered, as I pushed in. Just an inch, just the tip of me. She was wet, but she was tight—no matter her children, I got the feeling no one had ever been here before, like she was virginally waiting for me. I pulled back, and then pushed in again, playing my head against the tightness of her, waiting for her to loosen.

"A little deeper," she breathed.

I followed instructions, arching my hips forward incrementally. Still so damn tight. It made me want to push my entire cock inside her, to make her tight pussy hold me—but instead of losing control I moaned.

Her hips started moving now, and I realized she was experimenting. I went still, letting her play me, eyes closed as she felt her own power, sliding up and down.

My hands curled in the sheets by her head. "Has anyone ever told you how tight you are?"

"Is that good?" she asked, like a one-man woman.

"Very," I growled, as she slid herself off of me—and then right back on. Her hands reached up and pulled my hips lower and I waited as she writhed below me, pushing on and off, taking a little more of my cock in each time. I went down to my elbows on top of her, kissing her throat and neck, my chest against hers, our hips slowly matching until we were joined, and all of my cock was wrapped inside.

She moaned then, just like me, and we pulsed there, neither one of us wanting the other to go—me, conquering, her conquered, or maybe it was the other way around. Silent, our bodies rocked in time until she whispered, "More."

At that, I rose up, and began to thrust. We moved opposite now, apart-then-together, slow at first, then more quickly. Then her long legs wrapped around me, giving her pussy fully over.

What was her husband thinking, watching this show? I imagined him beating off beside a pump dispenser of lube into a fistful of tissues, although Fran being Fran it was probably classier than that. Still—as her eyes closed and her chin lifted, exposing her throat to me, as she began to moan more urgently—suddenly I wanted her. Just for me.

I leaned in and whispered into her ear. "Tell me what you want. Tell me what he's never done for you."

Her eyes opened and she stared. My hips didn't miss a beat, and I saw confusion pass over her face like a cloud—and then resolve. She pulled her hands up my back into my hair and brought my ear to her mouth.

"The wall. Take me on the wall."

The wall was a classic move in porn, because most female porn stars were the size of elves. But even though she was tall—I was strong. More than strong enough. I let my cock take my fill of her three more times, before pulling out and grabbing her, bodily.

I probably should've said something porny, like *'You're cumming with me now'* or *'Are those handcuffs, officer?'* But instead I made her stand, and together we stumbled over to the nearest wall, where I could practically feel the camera lenses pointed at my tat-covered back.

I took one of her hands, and planted it over her head, and then the other, pinning her there, as I kissed her again—and as she kissed me back, just as hard, her tongue searching my mouth. Then I reached down and grabbed one of her thighs, pulled it up, and then lowered my hips so I could slide back inside her.

She fought me, not to get away, but to participate, so I set her hands free—they touched every part of me, like she was worried I'd escape—and then I grabbed her ass with both hands.

"I've got you," I warned, and pulled her up.

She shouted in surprise, then her legs wound about me again, and we were how we'd been on the bed, only now here with me standing as she clung to me. She was solely at my mercy for each stroke, the depth and speed of penetration utterly controlled by my hands, wrapped around her ass the same way her pussy wrapped around my cock.

Her hands were over my shoulders and her mouth was near my neck where she kissed me until she started moaning. I pressed her into the wall, forcing her to feel all of me, grinding myself up against her as my hands pulled her down. Her moans had an urgent tone and were interspersed with words. "Yes—please—yes—more—yes," but I didn't need to hear them, I could read her body, feeling her ass clench and throb as she tried to thrust, feeling her pussy pull tighter still as it got ready to—

She shouted in my ear and her whole body spasmed, rocking on and off of me in wild accord. Her hips, trapped between me and the wall, bucked, and I groaned low, feeling the intensity of the life radiating off of her, feeding on the dark energy it gave me. "Yes," I growled, in perfect agreement, and thrust deep and hard two more times, making the waves of her orgasm milk my cock until I came, deep inside her.

I leaned against her then, felt and heard her heartbeat trembling in her breast. One of her hands fell limp and pounded the wall behind her, as if she were tapping out, and behind my back her feet untwisted. She set one down, as I slid out of her, then the other, and stood there, balanced by the wall, trembling like a leaf.

I nuzzled my head against hers, knowing soon the contact would be unwelcome, she would go back to her life, and I would go back to mine. "Do you think you made him happy?"

And I watched her face light up in the radiant way of one participating in true love. "Definitely," with a beaming smile, then kissed me.

AFTER THAT, I lay down naked on the bed, and watched her put her clothes on, humming cheerfully to herself. She didn't appear to feel used or degraded, not that I'd wanted those things, but I'd fully been expecting that—for her to have a freak out the second things were done. Instead, she was as cool as a mint green cucumber. Did she and her husband travel from town to town, accruing cuckold experiences? Maybe I was the degraded one.

"Thank you," she addressed me, once she was clothed, as primly as a mother at a PTA meeting. "That was fantastic."

"You're welcome, and I'm glad," I said, bemusedly.

She gave me an awkward low wave and then walked for the door, fishing her ring out of her pocket to put back on. I rocked back in the bed, awash in blood and sex. If only I could stay here tonight—but I couldn't, plus Sugar needed feeding.

I rocked out of bed and reached for borrowed jeans as Fran came in, crystal decanter in one hand and two matching glasses in the other.

"So?" I asked. I tugged my jeans up.

"Quite impressive." She held the bottle up. "Whiskey?"

"Please." I pulled the t-shirt on and sat on the edge of the bed. "Did, uh, everyone go home happy?"

"Oh yes. The wall thing was inspired."

"I can't take credit for it—she asked."

"Dirty girl," Fran clucked with a grin. She poured me a glass, handed it over, then sat down in the chair to pour herself one. "I was a little unsure at first, him being a para and all—"

"What?"

"He's a C5 para. We talked about it some beforehand. They've had all their children via IVF. Stop looking so horrified—I'm nothing if not accommodating, as you well know."

"I just—" I stammered.

"Don't worry, you didn't wreck anything. I have a sixth sense for these sorts of arrangements. Plus, they tipped you. People who don't leave happy don't tip."

There was no place on Fran's current outfit for her to hold cash or make change. She inspected a glamorous fingernail to ignore the look I was giving her and clucked. "I'm keeping it, because I'm charging you freezer rent. Also, if this happens again, I suspect they're going to want you to wear some sort of suit, and God knows you don't own one."

I gave up and laughed. "Whatever you say, Fran."

Her eyes flicked over and appraised me under fake lashes. "If only you meant that, Jack. But—a promise is a promise. You want to tell me why you showed up half-dead on my doorstep?" She reached up into her hair, where I heard the faint sound of clips giving away, then she took off her wig and set it on the decanter. "Because I'm all ears now."

I polished off the rest of the whiskey in my glass, poured myself another, and started talking.

FRAN LISTENED ATTENTIVELY. Good dommes were all about communication, and as Fran was one of the best, I felt truly listened to, a rarity in this town or any other.

"I just don't know what happened. I should've been able to slaughter him. No contest at all." My hand went for my ribs again. Danger was omnipresent, but pain? Only one other person had been able to hurt me since I'd become a vampire—my Mistress—and I didn't like the reminder.

"It's pretty obvious to me," Fran said, leaning back and recrossing her legs. "You already know you're not the only thing that goes bump in the night."

"Shit," I cursed. Fran was right. It was the obvious answer. I was just in denial.

"Sorry, Jack. I know how you feel about her." Fran said, and stood up with only a slight groan to give away how much her heels hurt— but when she looked down she was wincing on my behalf.

Because she knew the only other vampire I could ask for information was the one I hated and feared most—my Mistress, Rosalie.

"I'll keep the freezer running for you."

"Thanks," I said. I polished off the whiskey in my glass, setting it down. "And I'm keeping this jacket."

MEET JACK'S MISTRESS ROSALIE IN
BLOOD AT DUSK: DARK INK TATTOO BOOK TWO
READ ON FOR A SNEAK PEEK.

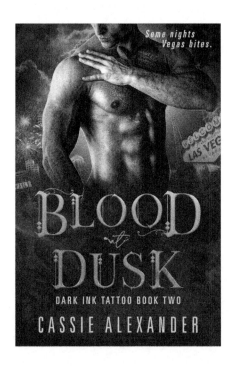

BLOOD AT DUSK
DARK INK TATTOO BOOK TWO
JACK

W hile your teenaged fantasies oftentimes involve bumping into teachers, former babysitters, and/or high-school head cheerleaders at the strip club, none of them—no matter how detailed—can prepare you for when it happens in real life. Which is why I was staring slack-jawed at Dorothy—*Thea*—as Bruce punched me in the arm.

"Jesus, when's the last time you saw a naked girl, Jack?"

I waved him away and kept staring. The runway was a long thing, phallically shaped, and we were at the tip of it while she was stage center near the pole, far enough away that it both could-and-couldn't be her simultaneously, like some Schrodingerian dream.

Bruce grabbed my head and yanked it near so he wouldn't have to shout over the music the club pumped in. "You're embarrassing yourself—and me."

She walked around the pole, looking out into likely darkness since all the lights were aimed at her, making all the sequins on her white bikini glint—it was like she was blindingly beautiful, too pretty to even see properly. Then she lunged forward and in, lifting herself up, long legs pointed in a dramatically suggestive V, ending in two glittering red platform heels, all the better to walk down a pornographic yellow brick road.

I turned toward him without taking my eyes off her. "I know her."

"The fuck you do."

But I did. I had a sudden flash of smoke and damage, a crinkle of red metal peeled up like wrapping paper on both sides of a tree and me running down to rescue her from the passenger side of a BMW, as quarterback Duncan Beamm staggered out on the driver side to puke, from a likely BAL of 0.3 and a head contusion.

Everything afterward.... "We're in Vegas. Bet me," I told Bruce, as she began a slow turn.

"A hundred."

"Done," I said. "Go hit the ATM."

He snorted and didn't move. Thea spun, the muscles of her arms, her stomach, the swing of her legs, making her swirl like a slow carousel. What was it like being up there with everyone watching? Rowdier groups of men waved fistfuls of cash, shouting lewd suggestions, and she ignored them, intent on her own internal metronome, letting the music move her. When it came time for her to take off her top it seemed natural and she swung down dramatically, one leg curving up to brace against the pole, the pink perfection of her nipples on display, swaying with the music like twin poppies.

How many times in high school had I desperately wanted to see those breasts—to touch them? The closest I'd ever come was that day in the rain, holding her to my chest, blood streaming out of a small cut on her cheek.

"THEA? THEA? ARE YOU OKAY?"

I was the first on the scene—they'd slalomed past me in the rain for no reason, and fishtailed over the edge of the road. I'd called it in on my way down the hill, leaving my truck parked on the shoulder up above for the ambulance to see.

I heard the sound of another puke on Duncan's side as Thea's eyelids fluttered. She sat up and took everything in then looked up at me.

"He has scholarships," she said, having done a mental calculation at the speed of light, far faster than I would've been able to.

"So?"

"Say I was driving."

"You weren't. He was, and he's an asshole." There were beer cans on the floor of her car, I could see them through the open door, beneath the fluttering tatters of airbags.

"Babe!" Duncan bellowed on the far side. "Babe, where'd you go?"

Thea wriggled free and stood with me close behind. "I'm here, baby, hang on—" she shouted, then turned to me. "Please, Jack."

We'd been in a few classes together, on and off, a group project here or there, but we both knew where we belonged. I was with the kids the other kids hated, the ones that listened to the wrong music and couldn't afford nice clothes, whereas Thea was some sort of angel, so light the rest of the cheerleading team picked her up to make her fly.

"Fuck his scholarships, Thea—he almost killed you."

She put her hands on my chest. "I know, okay? But it was an accident—and my dad's gonna kill me over this already—there's no reason to ruin his life too."

I had no love for Duncan or anyone else on the football team. But for Thea? I'd spent four years watching her in the halls, loving the way her skirts grazed the edges of the dress code, the way the Texas sun brought out tank tops that sometimes slipped to reveal brightly colored bras. I knew all of her classes after lunch and could identify her laugh at a hundred paces. And while I knew I could never be with her—I knew how high school worked, and those of us on the outside of it had a very clear view of the inside—there was no way I could deny her now.

"Babe!" Duncan shouted, finally standing higher than the hood, holding one hand to his head, reaching out to her with the other. "Come here, get away from that loser—"

"Shut up Duncan!" she shouted back, looking at me with tears welling in her eyes. We heard a siren in the distance and I stepped away from her.

"Only because you're asking." I jerked my chin at Duncan. "Fuck him."

"Fuck you," Duncan bellowed, charging two steps forward before toppling over.

She ran to his side, kneeling down, and then looked up at me. "Thank you," she whispered. I shrugged my shoulder like it didn't matter. The second the cops got there, I told them my story and drove off.

The next two weeks of school held a strange kind of magic for me. I'd see her in the halls, and she wouldn't look away. She gave me shy smiles, finally, at long last, noticing me—and making me feel that it was okay for me to notice her. She even came over and spoke to me at my locker, asking how I was doing, and we talked for long enough that one of my fellow 'losers' noticed and interrogated me afterwards.

But the week after that, a mere month before graduation, Duncan started a rumor that I'd driven them off the road—all the better excuse for half the football team to viciously beat me. I didn't dare go back to school, much less graduate—I left high school and that fucking small town and I never looked back.

KEEP READING

BLOOD AT DUSK: DARK INK TATTOO BOOK TWO!

AND BE SURE TO JOIN CASSIE'S MAILING LIST FOR SECRET SCENES, MORE CHARACTER ART, MERCHANDISE, AND EXTRA STORIES!

DARK INK TATTOO SERIES

Don't miss the rest of the Dark Ink Tattoo Series.

...with more to come!

ALSO BY CASSIE ALEXANDER

CHECK OUT CASSIEALEXANDER.COM FOR CONTENT/TRIGGER WARNINGS.

THE DARK INK TATTOO SERIES

Blood of the Pack

Blood at Dusk

Blood at Midnight

Blood at Moonlight

Blood at Dawn

Blood of the Dead *(January 2023)*

The Longest Night (Newsletter Bonus Story & Audio)

EDIE SPENCE SERIES

Nightshifted

Moonshifted

Shapeshifted

Deadshifted

Bloodshifted

TRANSFORMATION TRILOGY *(Coming early 2023)*

Bend Her

Break Her

Make Her

STANDALONE STORIES

AITA?

Her Ex-boyfriend's Werewolf Lover

Her Future Vampire Lover

The House

Rough Ghost Lover

WRITTEN WITH KARA LOCKHARTE

THE PRINCE OF THE OTHER WORLDS SERIES

Dragon Called

Dragon Destined

Dragon Fated

Dragon Mated

Dragons Don't Date (Prequel Short Story)

Bewitched (Newsletter Exclusive Bonus Story)

THE WARDENS OF THE OTHER WORLDS SERIES

Dragon's Captive

Wolf's Princess

Wolf's Rogue *(Coming soon)*

Dragon's Flame *(Coming soon)*

ABOUT THE AUTHOR

Cassie Alexander is a registered nurse and author. She's written numerous paranormal romances, sometimes with her friend Kara Lockharte. She lives in the Bay Area with one husband, two cats, and one million succulents.

Sign up for Cassie's mailing list here or go to cassiealexander.com/newsletter to get free books, bonus scenes, even more character art, and cat photos!

Printed in Great Britain
by Amazon

11049849R00102